Light Up New York

Other books by Natalie Grant

Glimmer Girls series

London Art Chase (Book One)

A Dolphin Wish (Book Two)

Miracle in Music City (Book Three)

Light Up New York

by Natalie Grant

with Naomi Kinsman

ZONDERKIDZ

Light Up New York
Copyright © 2017 by Natalie Grant
Illustrations © 2017 by Cathi Mingus

This title is also available as a Zondervan ebook.

Requests for information should be addressed to:
Zonderkidz, 3900 *Sparks Drive SE, Grand Rapids, Michigan 49546*

ISBN 987-0-310-75274-5

Art direction: Cindy Davis
Cover design and interior illustrations: Cathi Mingus
Content contributor: Naomi Kinsman
Interior design: Denise Froehlich

Printed in the United States of America

17 18 19 20 21 22 23 24 25 /DCI/ 20 19 18 17 16 15 14 13 12 11 10 9 8 7 6 5 4 3 2 1

To my Glimmer Girls—Gracie, Bella, and Sadie.
You're my greatest adventure. I love you.

Thank you to Naomi Kinsman for bringing your genius, creativity, and beautiful patience to this process. None of this would be a reality without you.

ONE

ia watched out her window as the cab rolled past the stone piers that supported the bridge. Between the crisscrossed steel beams, she caught glimpses of New York's tall buildings stretching into the sunset-colored sky. Even after all the Glimmer family adventures in the past few months, visiting New York City was a particularly special treat.

"It's like driving into a dragon's mouth!" Lulu shouted, bouncing in her booster seat.

Lulu had insisted on sitting in the middle of the cab's tiny back row, squished between Mia and Maddie. Mom and Dad had a row of their own in front of the girls, and Miss Julia sat alone in the row ahead of them.

"Watch your elbows, Lulu," Mia complained, exchanging a glance with Maddie.

Mia knew Maddie wouldn't say anything about Lulu nearly poking out her eye. Maddie might have been born on the same day as Mia, but their differences went far beyond Mia's glasses. Mia had been born two minutes earlier, was two inches taller, and her patience seemed to wear out two times faster. But lately, even Maddie's patience had been wearing thin. Whatever Mia and Maddie wanted to do, there was Lulu, insisting on being smack-dab in the middle of it.

"No wonder people call this city the concrete jungle," Miss Julia said, leaning forward and looking up out of the front window. "The bridge does feel like it's swallowing us up, doesn't it, Lulu? Oh, and girls, in case you're wondering, this is the Queensboro Bridge." After a moment of fact-checking on her phone, she added, "Built between 1901 and 1909."

Miss Julia was curious about everything, which was one of the things Mia liked best about traveling with their nanny. She made it feel like they had an on-the-go tour guide everywhere they went.

Lulu had been busy counting on her fingers, but now she looked up, eyes wide. "Whoa. That's more than a hundred years ago."

Maddie took hold of her seat belt strap and warily eyed the river below. "But the bridge is safe?"

"Actually, it was recently renovated," Miss Julia said. "They finished the renovation in 2012."

Someone leaned on their horn. Another car honked back, setting off a flurry of horns blaring on all sides.

"This traffic!" Dad said.

"Even when it's not rush hour, it's crowded," the cabbie said. "That's just the way the city is."

"It's often called the city that never sleeps," Mom said. "Which is one of the things I like most about New York. Also, there are, at the very least, 80 museums in the city. A great reason for another visit!"

Light Up New York

"Does that mean we don't have to sleep while we're here?" Lulu asked.

Dad laughed and reached back to tug on one of her pigtails. "Don't you wish."

"Speaking of sleep," the cabbie continued, making Mia wonder whether all New York cabbies were so talkative. At home, they hardly ever rode in cabs, but sometimes they did while on tour with Mom. Mia's favorite cabs were the ones they'd taken last summer in London, with steering wheels on the opposite side of the car. None of the London cabbies had spoken to them, though. Obviously, New York was different.

"Have you heard about the muckety-mucks who will be sleeping on the streets this Thursday night?" the cab driver went on. "They want to help homeless teens— that's a good thing. But I hope they know what they're getting themselves into. January in New York is cold. Good thing this week is well above zero and no snow yet . . . but still."

"Actually, I'll be singing at the Light Up New York concert on Friday night before the sleep-out," Mom said. "And so will the girls. We hear it's a beautiful event. Everyone streams into Times Square, candles lit, lighting up the surrounding streets. Last year, in the months after the event, hundreds of homeless teens transitioned off the streets."

"I'll sing you our song!" Lulu announced, and launched into it, filling the cab with her voice.

After an ear-splitting chorus and a verse, the cab-bie's radio crackled to life.

"Quiet now, Lulu," Mom said. "We need to make sure the driver can hear his radio."

"Huh," the cab driver said, eyeing Mom in the rear-view mirror. Mia could tell he wanted to ask Mom who, exactly, she was, but he left it alone.

Dad winked at Mom and laced his fingers through hers, whispering, "Muckety-muck."

Mia rolled the phrase around in her mind, wishing she could ask Miss Julia where it came from. Even though Mom was a muckety-muck—whatever that meant, exactly—thankfully, she wasn't going to sleep on the streets. Dad and the event organizers had decided Mom should sleep indoors to protect her voice. And that meant the girls wouldn't sleep outside either. Mia hoped she'd be bold enough to take part in the sleep-out when she was older, even though sleeping on the streets didn't sound one bit comfortable. If she'd learned one thing at Third Street Community House this fall, it was that being poor wasn't only about not having enough money. One of the worst parts of being poor was feeling less than others and separated from everyone else. Mia thought the sleep-out was an interesting way for the community to start to connect, even if it was only for one night.

"So, girls, we have a week in New York," Mom said. "What do you want to do while we're in the city?"

Mia reached for her journal. On the plane, she'd written a list of things she wanted to do. For the past few weeks, she'd been reading up on New York City and all there was to do here. But before Mia could even find the right page, Lulu threw both her arms into the air.

"Ice skate!" Lulu shouted. "Didn't you say we could ice skate outside?"

Mia blew out a sigh. Of course Lulu would want to ice skate. Lulu could skate rings around both her sisters, but especially Mia. Maddie was a pretty good skater too. It was all Mia could do to stay on her feet while her skates slipped and slid on the ice.

"Mia wrote a list on the plane." Maddie tapped Mia's half-opened journal. "You had a lot of good ideas."

"What sounds fun to you, Mia?" Mom asked.

Mia finished flipping through pages until she found the list. "Well, I read that the library isn't like ordinary libraries," she said. "There's art on display, which Maddie would like, and books, of course. And a map room."

She ran her finger down her list. "And there's the Met, where Claudia and her brother, Jamie, hid out and solved a mystery in *From the Mixed-Up Files of Mrs. Basil E. Frankweiler.* And they took a bath in the fountain and collected pennies."

"Who did what?" Lulu asked.

"They're characters in a book I read. It's by E. L. Konigsburg," Mia explained.

"Oooh!" Lulu grabbed hold of Mia and Maddie, so excited that her fingers dug into their arms. "That's what we should do! Solve a mystery!"

"Hold it." Dad turned to give them a serious look, but they could all see the smile under it. "I think we've had more than our share of mysteries for the year."

"You can say that again," Mom agreed. "Okay, so the library and the Metropolitan Museum of Art . . ."

"And ice skating!" Lulu said.

"And the Statue of Liberty," Maddie added.

"And I want to find the perfect cup of coffee," Dad said. "And eat some famous New York pizza."

"Pizza!!" Lulu echoed.

"I vote we have pizza for dinner," Mom said. "We'll get settled in our rooms and then go see what we can find. What do you say, girls?"

"Yay!" the girls chimed, for once in complete agreement.

"Here's your hotel," the cab driver said, pulling up to the curb and turning off the engine. "Welcome to the Grand Hyatt, ladies and gentleman."

TWO

Once through the revolving doors and past an indoor waterfall, the Glimmer family and Miss Julia rode the escalator up into the hotel lobby. Grand pillars lined either side of the wide open space. People sat on low, cushioned benches, which made the space look more like a waiting room than a lobby. Here and there, glass vases filled with white stones, curlicue sticks, and one or two bright orange flowers added a splash of color.

"Where's the front desk?" Maddie asked.

Mia couldn't immediately tell. Puzzled, she turned in a slow circle, taking in the concierge tables, the ballroom, and the bank of elevators. Finally, she saw people dressed in staff uniforms standing behind little counters on the left side of the room. For such a grand room, it was odd that the desk was almost disguised.

"This way," Dad said, leading the way toward the counters.

"Snacks!" Lulu made a beeline for the bright lights of the bakery that made up another corner of the lobby. She'd probably have piled her arms full of cookies and chips, but Miss Julia caught Lulu before she'd gone too far.

"Remember, we're going to have pizza in a few minutes," Mom said. "But it's good to know there are snacks right here in the lobby."

"Midnight snacks!" Lulu said.

"Maybe an apple or granola bar?" Mom's eyes twinkled. They all knew healthy snacks weren't what Lulu had meant.

After Dad had registered the Glimmers, the clerk behind the desk motioned to the escalator. "And just below the hotel is Grand Central Terminal. You'll find shops and restaurants down there, plus the subway and train systems that will take you anywhere you want to go."

He passed Dad the room keys and pointed out the elevators. "The two elevators closest to us only go to the lower floors. You'll want to take one of the others, which go all the way up to your rooms."

The elevator was so small that Mia wasn't sure everyone and all the luggage would fit. Finally, after they shuffled and stacked a couple bags, everyone managed to make it inside. A subway map lined one wall of the elevator. Mia studied it—so many colors, all indicating train routes going in all different directions. Street names labeled each stop rather than famous locations, so most of the station names didn't mean much to Mia. She did manage to pick out the large green square that made up Central Park and Yankee Stadium before the elevator pinged at floor 32.

"Everyone out!" Dad said, handing Miss Julia a key. "You're in room 3217, and we're right across the hall in 3216 and 3218."

Miss Julia rolled her suitcase to her room, promising to come to their rooms as soon as she settled in.

"We're in our own room?" Mia liked the idea of being more grown up, but she wasn't sure she and Maddie were grown up enough for their own room. Especially if they would have to look after Lulu and keep her out of trouble.

Mom wrapped an arm around Mia. "No, we're in adjoining rooms. There's a door between them that you can use at any time. We'll prop it open at night so you feel safe. I think we'll keep your room door bolted, so you can come in and out of our door. That way we can keep an eye on you."

Dad tickled Lulu and said, "Especially on YOU!"

Lulu giggled, and Mia felt better, but only slightly. The thing was, the last time they'd been in a big city, Lulu hadn't been the one to worry about. She'd made a little trouble, sure, but Maddie was the one who had snuck out without an adult. She'd had a reason— wanting to solve a mystery and feeling like no one was listening to her—but still.

Dad opened the door to his and Mom's room and flipped on the light. The Glimmers crowded into the little hallway between the bathroom and the closet. The room wasn't all that large. In fact, it was just big enough for a king bed with a bedside table on either side, a dresser with a TV on top, and a window seat.

"Is that the door to our room?" Lulu pointed to a door beside one of the bedside tables.

"I think so." Dad tried the handle and then pushed it open.

The girls all piled through to a room that was almost identical to their parents' room. Mia stopped short when she saw one king bed.

"We're all supposed to sleep in one bed?"

"No, one of you is going to sleep on a rollaway," Mom said.

"You mean one of those little beds on wheels?" Mia asked. "I want to sleep on it!"

"No, I want to!" Lulu said. "I want my own bed."

Mom held up her hands before the girls could launch into a full-blown argument. "How about we decide after we've had some pizza? Let's put your bags in the closet so we don't trip over them. Later, we'll unpack and settle in, since we'll be here for a week."

As Mom helped Lulu stack the bags in the closet, Maddie pulled open the blinds. "Look!"

Outside, buildings loomed. It was a little strange not to be looking up or down at them. Even all the way up there on the thirty-second floor, they were right in the middle of everything. Across the street, Mia could see into lit windows, like she was looking through frames at moving pictures. People at desks answered phones and filed papers and rolled around in rolling chairs.

"They have no idea we're watching them," Mia said.

"Maybe someone is watching us back!" Maddie said, and they both ducked, peeking over the window frame to scan the building for anyone who might be looking out.

"What are you doing?" Lulu asked, joining them.

Mia's hands balled into fists. Every time she and Maddie were finally having some time just for them, Lulu snuck in.

"We're just playing around," Maddie said, noticing Mia's frustration and trying, as usual, to smooth things over. "Pretending someone might be watching us, the way we're watching them."

Dad popped his head into the room. "Ready for pizza?"

"Yes!" Mia's stomach growled, and she knew that some food would take her mind off Lulu.

The girls leapt to their feet, nearly knocking into one another in their excitement.

"Pizza!" Lulu shouted, twirling her way out the door. "Pizza, pizza, pizza!"

THREE

After bundling back into hats and gloves, they knocked on Miss Julia's door. She had already made her room her own. She'd stacked her books on the bedside table, arranged a collection of winter hats up on the desktop, and hung her clothes neatly in the closet. She'd left her fuzzy slippers beside the bed.

The girls helped Miss Julia choose a striped hat for the pizza trip, and then they rode the elevator down to the lobby. The restaurant was several blocks away, but not too far to walk. At each crosswalk, a flood of cars passed. Taxis swooped around cars that weren't moving fast enough . . . or so the taxi drivers thought. The screech of tires and honking of horns filled the air. Even before the crosswalk light changed, people poured out into the street. Mia feared for their lives, but fortunately, most cars yielded to pedestrians.

The city was alive with people—people on bikes, in cars, on buses, and walking. Business people hurried along in groups, deep in conversation. People walked handfuls of dogs, and vendors shouted about the food in their carts. Parents with strollers tried to keep track of their other kids, who stopped in the middle of the sidewalk to look up without warning. Mia found herself doing the same. Everywhere she looked, the city was a jumble of interesting sights. Scaffoldings surrounded construction projects. Trees filled postcard-sized parks. Every once in a while, something took her breath away, like the soaring spires of a cathedral. After a few blocks, Miss Julia circled around to walk behind the girls and make sure none of them got left behind.

"How many people live in this city, anyway?" Mia asked Miss Julia.

"Eight point four six million," Miss Julia answered after consulting her phone.

"And what's that super tall building over there?" Maddie asked, pointing out a building that rose above all the rest, with a tall spike on top.

"That's the Empire State Building," Miss Julia said. "It's one of the tallest buildings in New York, but One World Trade Center is taller. I'm sure we'll see that one too, while we're here."

Mia's nose had turned red and her glasses had fogged up by the time Dad pulled open the door to the restaurant. Warm air billowed out, filled with the smell of oregano and tomato sauce. They piled inside, and a waiter led them up a spiral staircase to the second floor, where an empty table waited.

He passed around menus. "Remember to save room for the cannoli."

"New York pizza," Dad breathed, eyeing the menu.

"Is it different from other pizza?" Maddie wanted to know.

"Usually, New York pizza crust is thin and crispy," Dad said. "And they make it in a brick pizza oven. I think we should get one pepperoni and one tomato basil."

"Sounds good to me!" Mom's phone rang, and she checked the screen. "Excuse me a moment."

Mia tried to listen without Mom noticing. She wasn't supposed to eavesdrop, but detectives needed great listening skills. Ever since she and her sisters had started solving mysteries, she'd become more and more curious. For instance, she liked to guess what was happening on the other side of phone conversations, based on the hints she could hear. Except right now, Mia couldn't hear a thing. Lulu drowned everything out, describing a new episode in the fairy story she'd been writing all year. This time, the telling included sound effects.

"Shh, Lulu!" Mia scolded.

Lulu stuck out her tongue, but was quiet long enough for Mia to hear Mom for a moment.

"We're so grateful for the opportunity," Mom was saying. "May I think it over and get back to you tomorrow morning?"

Think what over? Mia's mind filled with possibilities. She kept listening, hoping to pick up more hints. Since Lulu had cued into Mom's conversation now as well, at least Mia could finally hear. They all waited while Mom said good-bye.

When she had put the phone away, Dad raised a questioning eyebrow. "Opportunity?"

"I'll tell you about it later," Mom said.

"What it is, what is it, what is it?" Lulu clasped her hands and gave Mom her sweetest "tell me" look.

"Later." Mom wore her most serious "I mean it" look.

"Are we ready to order?" the waiter asked, arriving at the table again with pad and pen in hand.

Mia was grateful for his excellent timing. Lulu pouted, but didn't push further. She launched back into her telling of the fairy story, and Mia tried to pretend it didn't bother her that no one could get a word in edgewise. Mia kept a close watch on Mom, wondering about the mysterious opportunity. If it had been an opportunity for her or Dad, she'd have just told them. That meant the opportunity might be for the girls. Mia decided to be on her best behavior all through dinner, just in case that would make a difference. If there was an opportunity, she didn't want to ruin it by snipping at Lulu.

Miss Julia leaned close to talk to Mia without interrupting Lulu. "You know, I saw a little bookstore on our way over tonight. I was thinking it might be fun to pick up a copy of *From the Mixed-Up Files of Mrs. Basil E. Frankweiler* to read while we're here in the city."

"Can we?" Mia asked, completely distracted from her thoughts for a moment. *From the Mixed-Up Files* was one of her favorite books. "Ooh, and maybe we can make up a mystery of our own to solve when we go to the Met. Like a scavenger hunt or something from the book."

"It wouldn't be a trip without a mystery to solve," Maddie agreed.

Soon, the pizzas arrived, and Lulu was too busy eating to tell stories. Mia kept thinking about the possible opportunity, and about being on her best behavior. She didn't even snap at Lulu when her little sister snatched the last piece of pepperoni pizza before anyone else could get it. Dad seemed to notice, and gave Mia first choice of cannoli. She'd never had one before, and discovered, to her delight, that they were sweet and creamy on the inside and crunchy on the outside. Maddie decided her favorite part was the maraschino cherries on each end. Of course, Lulu liked the tiny chocolate chips the best.

"Ready to walk back?" Dad asked after the bill was paid.

Lulu hopped out of her seat. "Can we watch television in bed?"

"We'll see," Mom said, and led the way down the stairs toward the street.

ia hung back to walk with Maddie. If they put their heads together, they might come up with an idea of what this mysterious opportunity might be. After a block or two of batting around possibilities, they hadn't made much progress. So they settled into the conversation they'd been having on and off for weeks, about how to sell as many albums as possible. Earlier this fall, Mia and Maddie had made friends with a girl named Ruby, who lived at Third Street Community House. Before meeting Ruby, Mia hardly knew anything about homelessness. But through a series of events, they'd ended up putting on a concert with Ruby to raise funds to help her dad buy a guitar. After that, they'd seen Ruby about once a week, even after she and her family moved into a regular apartment. Ruby had asked Mia and Maddie whether they might record an album together. She wanted to raise funds for teenagers living on the streets.

"No one should be homeless," Ruby had said. "But teens, especially. Homeless teens are usually all on their own, and it seems like they're in the most danger of anyone. I just want to do something to help."

Mia hadn't ever considered recording an album of their own, but once they started really thinking about it, she realized they had everything they needed to make it work. For one thing, Dad had the basement studio where he could record the whole album. Plus, Dad could compose the arrangements, and he knew all about how to put albums together. Once the ball started rolling, things fell into place quickly. They got help from Dad, and Mom even asked some of her band members to help. Soon, what seemed like a crazy idea had come together.

"What are you talking about?" Lulu wanted to know as she joined the twins.

Mia answered before stopping to think. "The album."

"You're always leaving me out!" Lulu wailed, stomping off to take Miss Julia's hand.

Mia sighed, and Maddie didn't say anything at all. At first, Lulu had wanted to be part of the Sparkle and Shine album project, but she didn't have the patience to stick with it. Still, they'd included her in one song. Even so, every time she heard them talking about the album, she acted like the entire project made her feel left out.

"She'll get over it," Maddie said, linking elbows with Mia.

"I hope so," Mia said, not feeling all that hopeful.

They stopped at the bookstore and found *From the Mixed-Up Files*. Miss Julia bought it as a present for all the girls and promised to read them a bit every day while they were in New York City. On their way through the hotel lobby, they used the fun touchscreen camera to take a family photo and post it online. Immediately, one of Mom's fans commented, "Light up New York, Glimmer family!"

All through the elevator ride, Mom's phone pinged with likes and comments.

"Is this the first Light Up New York Week, Mom?" Mia asked.

"The sleep-out event has been going on for a few years," Mom said. "But this is the first year there's been a citywide Light Up New York Week."

"So what are people supposed to do?" Maddie asked.

"Kind things," Mom said.

"Like sparkling and shining?" Lulu asked.

"That's right," Mom said, smiling.

"The Glimmer girls motto is catching!" Miss Julia said.

"Sparkle and shine, but most of all, be kind!" the girls chanted as the elevator doors pinged open.

"Shh!" Mom pointed out the quiet hours sign. "People might be sleeping."

Mia put her finger to her lips, and then the girls whispered together, "Sparkle and shine, but most of all, be kind!"

They hugged Miss Julia good night and then followed Mom and Dad into their rooms. Mia was first through the adjoining door. While they had been gone, someone had delivered the rollaway, leaving it in the space between the bed and the window. Mia flopped onto it, bouncing on her knees, trying the mattress out for softness.

"So, I get the rollaway?" Lulu asked, pushing Mia aside, nearly knocking her onto the floor.

Mia stood up, grumbling under her breath. Maddie caught her hand and squeezed it.

"No!" Mia said, the word bursting out of her before she could stop it. "Lulu always gets what she wants, just because she's the youngest."

"It's not true. I don't get everything I want." Lulu's eyes filled up with tears. "I don't get *anything* I want."

She flung herself onto the rollaway as though she was a heroine in an old-fashioned movie, and sobbed into the pillow. Mia wasn't so sure she wanted to sleep on that bed now that Lulu was sniffling and snuffling all over it. Still, it was the principle of the thing. Lulu acted like she didn't get anything she wanted when the truth was, she almost always got her way. She cried and made a scene, and then the easiest thing for anyone to do was to give in and let her have what she wanted.

"Stop crying!" Mia snapped.

Mom came in, her forehead creased with concern. "What's going on?"

"Lulu's crying again," Mia said. "But she's the one who pushed me off the rollaway. I didn't do anything to her."

Maddie didn't speak up, but for once, Mia could see that she agreed with her. Thank goodness. Even Maddie had her limits.

"Girls," Mom said. "Tonight, we're going to give Lulu the rollaway." Before Mia could protest, Mom added,

"But not because she's crying. Trust me on this, Mia, something special is coming, and I think you will eventually agree that it's fair for Lulu to have the rollaway."

Lulu's sobs stopped as suddenly as they'd started. She hopped off the bed, ran over, and pulled on Mom's arm. "I don't want my own bed anymore. I want something special."

"We'll talk more after I discuss the situation with Dad, but for now, the rollaway is yours, Lulu."

Lulu eyed Mom, and then the rollaway, then back at Mom again. She plopped down on the small bed and pulled a pillow into her lap, cocking her head at Mia with a "Win for me!" look.

Mia bit back her response and her questions. She knew the special something must have to do with the "opportunity" from the earlier phone call. One look at Maddie's face told her that her sister was thinking the same thing. She wasn't sure if it was because they were twins, or because they were sisters, but sometimes, it truly did seem like she could read Maddie's mind.

"Now, it's time for pjs and then bed," Mom said. "Tomorrow, I know you'll want lots of energy for exploring New York."

"And for ice skating!" Lulu reminded her. "But can we watch one show while we fall asleep? Please? Since we're in a hotel?"

"If you can find a show all three of you agree on, you can watch it while you fall asleep," Mom said.

From the other room, Dad made his *hum . . . hum . . . hummm . . .* sounds, and then he slid through the door in full Tickle Monster mode. He tickled Lulu and Maddie and then Mia and then Maddie again.

"Me, me!" Lulu shrieked, and then when Dad pounced to tickle her, she could barely say, "Stop!" over her breathless giggles.

Mia's smile lasted, even through the choosing of the show. Lulu insisted on *Dancing with the Stars*, which wasn't Mia's favorite, but she didn't mind it all that much. She curled up on the pillows, closed her eyes, and let the sounds of the television fade into the background.

God, she found herself praying. *Make me just a little more patient tomorrow.*

FIVE

When Mia opened her eyes, the room was still dark. She wasn't sure if it was actually still dark outside, or if their room was just darkened because the blind was down. Maddie and Lulu were still asleep. Quietly, Mia slipped out of bed and tiptoed into her parents' room.

"Good morning," Mom whispered, scooting over to make room for Mia. "Are your sisters up?"

"Not yet." Mia cuddled up with Mom on the bed.

"Dad's taking a shower," Mom said, setting her coffee mug aside. "But I'm glad you're here, because I wanted to talk to you."

"About the opportunity?" Mia could hear the hopeful tone in her own voice.

"You know I'm scheduled to appear on *Rise and Shine* tomorrow to promote the sleep-out and concert?"

"Yes . . ." Mia said, her breath catching in her throat.

"Well, the exciting news is that the producer invited you and Maddie to join me. The guest they'd scheduled to come on after me had to cancel last minute, so they wanted to extend my interview. Since you girls are raising money with your new album, they thought it would be perfect if you would come talk about the project."

Mia could hardly sit still. She looked up at Mom with giant eyes.

Mom grinned and nodded. "Mmm-hmm! What do you think?"

"Yes!" Mia said. It was all she could do to keep her voice a whisper. "Yes, yes, yes!"

"But . . ." Mom said, and Mia's stomach sank. She already knew what Mom would say next.

"Lulu," Mia said, looking down at her hands unhappily.

"We decided this album would be for you, Maddie, and Ruby," Mom said. "And I think that was the right decision. Plus, I was proud of how you featured Lulu in one song so she wouldn't feel completely left out."

"She wouldn't have been able to focus on the album for all those rehearsals," Mia said.

"I know," Mom agreed. "Like I said then, this project is something that God put on your and Maddie's hearts."

"And Ruby's!" Mia added.

"Yes," Mom said. "As you and your sisters grow up, situations like this will happen more and more. Different projects will interest you, and sometimes the best way to support each other is to cheer one another on."

"Even for me and Maddie?"

"You've already seen how that can happen, haven't you?" Mom asked. "You love learning about animals and reading, and Maddie loves drawing. Both of you love music, but Maddie doesn't always love to perform."

"What's happening?" Maddie asked, appearing in the doorway.

"Good morning!" Lulu said, pushing past Maddie and taking a flying leap onto the bed.

Mom pulled them all into a big hug. "Let's talk about our plans for the day."

Lulu scrambled up onto her knees. "Ice skating!"

"Actually, yes," Mom said, catching Mia's eye before she could object. "Lulu, Daddy and I are taking you skating this morning."

Maddie tilted her head, confused. "Just Lulu?"

"Daddy and I decided Lulu should have a special treat today because you and Mia are going to have a special treat tomorrow," Mom said.

"What treat?" Maddie asked.

"Last night, the phone call you were all so interested in was from a producer. I'm scheduled to appear on *Rise and Shine* tomorrow morning," Mom said. "But, Maddie, they'd like you and Mia to come on the show with me so that you can talk about your album."

"What?" Lulu wailed. "Without me?"

"You do get to sit in the audience with Miss Julia," Mom said. "But that's why we wanted to take you ice skating today—so you could have a treat of your own."

Honestly, Mia was relieved she wouldn't have to skate. A disaster avoided, and she and Maddie would get to be on television. Television!

"I called a salon for you girls," Mom said. "It's definitely time for a haircut, and they will also do a pretty blowout for you both. Miss Julia can take you while we skate. Sound okay?"

Maddie nodded, looking just as happy as Mia felt.

"What about my hair?" Lulu demanded.

"I suppose you could choose to go to the hair salon instead of going skating," Mom said.

"Instead?" Lulu asked, giving Mom one of her signature "pretty, pretty please" looks.

Mom raised her eyebrows, and Mia was happy to see she wasn't affected in the least. "Yes. Instead. If it were up to me, I'd choose to skate with you. I'd like to have a special treat, just for us. But if you choose to have your hair done with your sisters, that's your choice to make. It's important that you understand. If you choose not to ice skate now, we won't go skating at another time on this trip."

"Plans all settled?" Dad asked, poking his head out of the bathroom.

"Nearly," Mom said. "What do you think, Lulu?"

"I want to do both, *and* be on television," Lulu said, pouting.

Mom nodded. "I understand. If you aren't able to change your attitude, though, you won't be able to have any special treats."

"Okay, okay! Skating!" Lulu said, clearly realizing she was on thin ice.

Mia couldn't help wondering how long the good attitude would last. Would Lulu honestly sit quietly in the television studio audience?

"I'll be ready in a minute," Dad said.

"We'll go check on Miss Julia," Mom said. "Well . . . after the girls get dressed."

"And after we brush our teeth!" Maddie said.

Soon, they were all dressed, with faces washed, teeth cleaned, and hair brushed. Mia was grateful they'd be getting their hair cut and styled. Lately, when she fixed her hair, it seemed to do the opposite of what she wanted it to do. Television. She could hardly wait.

✳ ✳ ✳

There was a small outdoor skating rink in a park within walking distance from the hotel. The minute Lulu had her skates on, she launched herself onto the ice. Mom and Dad had to hurry to catch up, and soon they were all gliding across the ice. Mia tried not to be jealous as she stood next to Maddie and Miss Julia, watching. If only she could skate like that. Lulu raised her hand to wave, and wobbled a little on her skates, making Mia feel slightly better. Then, guilt swept through her. Why did she sometimes have such unkind thoughts when it came to Lulu? It wasn't that she didn't want good things for her little sister. It was just so hard when it seemed Lulu tried to ruin things for Mia and Maddie. But this

time, so far, so good. Lulu hadn't put up too much of a fuss about the *Rise and Shine* appearance.

"We should probably go." Miss Julia checked the time on her phone. "Bubblegum Suds is a few blocks away, and our appointment is in about ten minutes."

"Bubblegum Suds?" Maddie asked.

Miss Julia shook her head. "With a name like that, I can't wait to see what this salon looks like."

Mia took Miss Julia's hand in one of her gloved hands, and Maddie's in the other. "We're going to be on television, Maddie! Can you believe it?" Finally, she didn't have to stuff down her excitement so she wouldn't hurt Lulu's feelings. Television!

Maddie squeezed Mia's hand back. She wasn't bouncing out of her skin like Mia, but she also wasn't instantly worried. A few months ago, she would have panicked about appearing on television. Maddie had changed a lot since last summer, starting with the trip to London, and then when she'd performed in the bene-fit at the Grand Ole Opry this fall. Mia wondered if she, personally, had changed as much as her sister. Then she remembered how upset she'd been this summer about all the ways Maddie was changing. Just the fact that she was proud of her sister now was definitely a change. Like Mom said, just because they were sisters didn't mean they had to do every single thing together. And then, when they did choose to do something together, like the album, being together made the project all the more fun.

"Ruby!" Maddie said, stopping right in the middle of the sidewalk.

"We haven't told her!" Mia said, picking up on Maddie's unspoken thought.

"She'll be excited, won't she?" Maddie asked. "I mean, she won't feel left out?"

"She might . . ." Mia thought about how Ruby might feel. Then she added, "But we can mention her. You know she'll just be excited that so many people will hear about the album."

"We'll have to call her after your hair appointments," Miss Julia said. "Because we're here!"

SIX

Black-and-white stripes and polka dots filled Bubblegum Suds salon. Pink highlights broke up the pattern—a pillow or throw rug, a border on a mirror.

"Welcome to Bubblegum Suds, ladies." The receptionist stood to greet them. "You must be the Glimmer girls."

Mia wondered for a split second if they were starting to become famous. They had recorded an album and now were going to be on *Rise and Shine*. But then she realized Mom had made an appointment for them. Of course the receptionist was expecting them. Mia rearranged her look of surprise into what she hoped was a more appropriate, ordinary smile. With any luck, the receptionist wasn't quick to read thoughts on other people's faces. And hopefully, Maddie and Miss Julia had been too busy saying hello to have noticed.

"These are for you." The receptionist handed over black-and-white-striped smocks with pink sashes folded neatly on top.

She pointed them toward the dressing rooms and also pointed out two empty chairs across the room. "After you're changed, Rhea and Walden will be your stylists. You can meet them over there."

Mia wasn't sure what the woman meant by changing, but it must have something to do with the smocks.

She'd never had to change when she went to the hair salon back home.

Miss Julia ushered them toward the dressing rooms and explained. "Hang your shirts on a hanger, girls, and then put on the smocks."

"Why?" Maddie asked.

"Keeps you from getting pieces of hair caught in your clothes," Miss Julia said.

"That *is* itchy," Mia pointed out.

They changed, then crossed the salon and climbed up into their side-by-side chairs.

"I'm Rhea," said the woman behind Mia's chair. Like Mia, she wore glasses, but hers were small and rectangular, with bright blue frames. Rhea had matching blue streaks scattered through her layered black hair.

"And I'm Walden," the other woman said, and fluffed Maddie's hair. "Let me guess. You want hot pink highlights."

Maddie eyed Walden's spiky hair, each spike tipped with lime green. Walden laughed, the kind of laughter that made Mia feel much more comfortable.

"I'm kidding." Walden checked her notes. "Your mom said a trim and a blowout. We'll make you beautiful for *Rise and Shine* tomorrow. Shall we go wash your hair?"

Mia and Maddie followed the stylists to the wash basins. Miss Julia went back to the reception area to wait. Mia soaked the experience in—the warm water flowing through her hair, the jasmine smell of the shampoo, the fluffy towel Rhea wrapped around her head after the washing was done.

As they made their way back to their chairs, Mia realized the mood in the salon had changed. Excitement fizzled and sparked across the room. The receptionist and Miss Julia stood by the window, watching something happening outside.

"What's going on?" Mia asked.

Instead of climbing into her chair, Maddie stood on her tiptoes, trying to see. "It's a news camera, I think."

"Probably the Snow Angel again," Rhea said.

"The who?" Maddie asked.

"Climb on up, and we'll tell you," Walden said.

Mia watched in the mirror as Rhea unwrapped her hair. It tumbled down around her shoulders in damp clumps.

Rhea spritzed Mia's hair with a sweet-smelling vanilla spray and then started pulling a comb through. "About three weeks ago, someone started leaving little gifts for people around the city. With each gift, they left a paper snowflake."

"Maybe it started even earlier than that," Walden said. "No one really knows."

"The thing is," Rhea continued, warming to the topic as she took out her scissors and started to snip, "you'd think the Snow Angel would want credit for all the good things he's doing."

"Or she," Walden put in.

"Or she," Rhea agreed. "But for whatever reason, the Snow Angel has kept his or her identity secret."

"I'm sure the mystery is the reason the whole thing has captured so much attention," Walden said.

"What kind of gifts?" Maddie asked.

"Blankets, shoes, thick socks, groceries. One time, the Snow Angel left a Red Rider wagon for a homeless woman. Up to that point, the woman had to lug around her possessions in soggy bags."

"And remember the birthday cake?" Walden asked.

"There was this old man who lived in a tiny walk-up, all by himself. And he always kept to himself. In fact, all his neighbors said he was the kind of man who would snap at you for the tiniest of things. But on his birthday, the Snow Angel left him a birthday cake on his front stoop. With candles."

"That's why it's been so hard for everyone to figure out who the Snow Angel might be," Rhea said. "The gifts show up all over town, so we can't pin down where he might live or work."

"And the gifts aren't random," Walden added. "They're specific to each person. The Snow Angel seems to know each of the people who receive the gifts, or at least knows something important or personal. But how could one person know so many random people all over town?"

"A mystery," Maddie said, catching Mia's eye.

"One that everyone in the city has been trying to solve for weeks now," Walden said.

Mia knew exactly what Maddie was thinking. Unlike a scavenger hunt around the Met, this was a real live mystery. Looking for clues and solving puzzles made exploring new places more fun. What's more, the Glimmer girls had proved themselves to be excellent detectives. What if they could solve a mystery that not even well-trained New York reporters could solve?

"Do they have any guesses about who the Snow Angel might be?" Mia asked, trying not to be too obvious as she slipped into clue-gathering mode.

"There are theories, of course. Some people think it's a philanthropist who wanted to give his or her money away in a more personal way."

"Or a brand, like Coca-Cola, who will eventually claim the giving spree as a marketing campaign."

"I hope it's not a big brand," Rhea said. "Can't someone just be doing all this from the goodness of her heart?"

"Maybe . . ." Walden's mouth rose in a half smile. "But probable?"

The question lingered in the air as Rhea and Walden took out hair dryers and started them up. Section by section, Mia's hair smoothed out and curled under at the ends. Even though Rhea had styled Mia's hair close to the way she wore it every day, the extra attention made it glossy and light and full of body.

Walden blew Maddie's hair dry with a little curl in it. Hopefully their hair would stay this way, even when they slept on it tonight.

Finally, Rhea and Walden turned the hair dryers off and spun Maddie and Mia's chairs so they could see the backs of their heads.

"I love it!" Maddie said.

"Me too," Mia said.

"Off you go, then. And break a leg tomorrow," Rhea said, glancing over to check with Walden. "That's what you say for TV, right? Break a leg, like in the theater."

Walden shrugged. "Sounds good to me."

Mia and Maddie waved, and after Miss Julia paid, they headed out the door.

"Off to Serendipity," Miss Julia said. "We're meeting everyone for frozen hot chocolate!"

SEVEN

When Mia saw the Serendipity sign up ahead, she caught Maddie's arm. "Should we tell Lulu about the Snow Angel?"

They'd discussed the case all the way from Bubblegum Suds, and Mia's mind raced with ideas. As tourists, they'd have tons of opportunities to look for clues all over the city. And now that she and her sisters had solved three mysteries in less than a year, Mia felt like an expert. Plus, the Snow Angel mystery was all fun, no danger. Mom and Dad wouldn't have any reason to worry, would they? The only trouble was Lulu. What if she made the mystery yet another way to grab all the attention for herself?

"She'll find out." Maddie shook her head. "The minute she notices us looking for clues, she'll know we have a secret. You know she'll be curious. Crazy curious. Maybe the mystery will be like the album project. Maybe she'll lose interest as soon as we include her."

"Maybe," Mia said, but she wasn't convinced.

"Coming, girls?" Miss Julia asked, waiting in Serendipity's doorway.

The minute Miss Julia opened the door, the warm chocolate smell curled around the girls, drawing them inside the New York City restaurant that was famous for its desserts.

"Yum," Maddie sighed, as they made their way across the room to the table where Mom, Dad, and Lulu were already sitting, waiting.

"Serendipity is famous for frozen hot chocolate," Mom said as the girls and Miss Julia walked up.

"Wait, how can it be frozen and hot?" Mia asked.

Dad winked. "Let's order some and find out."

As he headed toward the counter, the girls slid into the booth opposite Mom and Lulu.

"I did a double twirl!" Lulu said, nearly bursting with her news. "And people clapped!"

"She was pretty amazing," Mom acknowledged, then tilted her head one way and then another, studying Mia's and Maddie's hair. "And it looks like you had a successful trip too. Your hair is beautiful, girls."

"Mmph." Lulu tugged on Mom's arm. "I want to get my hair done! You said I get to be in the audience for *Rise and Shine*. Maybe they'll call me up on stage!"

"Lulu, remember what we talked about," Mom said.

Mia could tell this must have been a long conversation, and one that Lulu hadn't liked much. Lulu pouted, her struggle to hold back all the things she'd like to say clear on her face. In the end, she couldn't completely hold back. "Well, I'm on the album too."

But just in one song . . . Mia managed to bite her tongue and not say this aloud. Just then, Dad returned with the most giant glass ever, filled with something chocolate and whipped cream, and six spoons.

"I figured we only needed one of these monsters," Dad said.

"Whoa!" Lulu breathed.

Everyone took a bite, and for a moment, no one said anything at all. The chocolate was creamy and delicious. Mia couldn't wait to take another bite, and another, but it was so rich that she couldn't eat it fast. She took her time with each bite, savoring the chocolaty goodness.

Finally, after a few bites, Lulu broke the silence. "Yummmmm."

Everyone nodded, and then burst out laughing. Around the table, everyone wore the exact same "I'm in chocolate bliss" smile.

After a couple more bites, Maddie said, "Lulu, guess what?"

"Hmm?" Lulu asked, looking up from her spoon.

"While we were at Bubblegum Suds, we heard about a New York mystery. Mia and I think the Glimmer girls should solve the case!"

"Wait a second . . ." Dad started.

"Not a dangerous mystery," Mia was quick to add. "There's this person who's been leaving gifts all over the city, and with them, a paper snowflake. Everyone's calling this person the Snow Angel and trying to figure out who the person is. But so far, the Snow Angel's identity is a total mystery."

Mom's face lit up. "I love that! The Snow Angel!"

"We saw reporters outside Bubblegum Suds . . . What were they doing, exactly, Miss Julia?" Maddie asked.

"Interviewing some people from the neighborhood. Someone had received a snowflake gift nearby. The reporters hoped someone in the neighborhood might have seen the Snow Angel. Or at the very least, hoped someone had seen something unusual that could help them solve the mystery of the Angel's identity."

"But no one had?" Mom asked.

"No," Miss Julia said. "While I was waiting for the girls, I watched some of the other Snow Angel interviews on my phone. Whoever the Snow Angel is, he or she is extremely sneaky. Even after three weeks of gift-giving, no one has any idea who he or she might be."

"Odd." Dad frowned at his spoon, and then dug in for another bite. "But it's wonderful that, for once, the breaking news is actually good news."

"So it's okay for us to take the case?" Mia asked.

"Take the case, huh?" Dad asked. "Soon, we're going to have to print business cards for you girls."

"Glimmer Girls Detective Agency," Lulu said, and launched into the theme song she'd composed back in London.

"As long as you remember we are here to have fun on this trip," Mom said. "Mysteries have a way of taking over. And remember, girls, you have *Rise and Shine* tomorrow too. We already have a lot going on."

"But looking for clues is fun," Maddie said. "It makes you look more closely at things, the way an artist might."

"That's true . . ." Mom said.

"And we wouldn't be putting ourselves in any kind of danger," Mia said. "This is just a fun puzzle to solve."

Miss Julia eyed each one of them in turn. "And you promise there will be no running off?"

"We promise!" Lulu thumped her fist on the table, making all the spoons jump with a clatter. "So, where do we look for clues?"

Mia tried not to sigh as a little of her excitement sizzled out. *God, what's wrong with me?* she asked silently. *Why can't I just be happy that Lulu is happy?*

Sometimes she wished God would answer immediately and in a way that was easy to understand. She knew prayer wasn't like rubbing a genie lamp. God had reasons for answering right away sometimes, and for waiting at other times. But for what seemed like forever, God had been silent when it came to Lulu. A lot of the time, when Mia knew she had an attitude that wasn't right, she could work hard and fix it. But with Lulu, even though Mia knew how she wanted to feel in her mind, a lot of the time, her heart didn't cooperate.

"We thought we could start by researching where the Snow Angel left each of the gifts," Maddie said. "Maybe mark them on a map and see if we notice anything, like a pattern."

"That's smart thinking," Dad said. "We can pick up a New York City map on the way home."

"Will you help us look up a list of the gifts, Miss Julia?" Mia asked.

"You bet!" she said, taking out her phone. "Sounds like the perfect job for me."

"Let's go now, then, and get started!" Lulu said.

They took the last bites of their frozen treat, and then bundled up to head back to the hotel.

EIGHT

Even though the girls were anxious to start working on their map, making it back to the hotel took forever. First, Dad took them on a detour to try out a coffee shop.

"What do you think?" Mom had asked.

"Maybe a 7 out of 10," Dad said. "We'll have to keep looking."

"The map!" the girls insisted.

So, they had gone into a gift shop and found a map of the city and some postcards to send home. Across the street from the gift shop, Dad noticed another coffee shop he wanted to try. While he and Mom went in to taste another cappuccino, Miss Julia took the girls into an art store nearby. The girls decided to choose a red pen for marking up their map. They found one with a thick felt tip, and decided it was perfect. Maddie went through the shop aisle by aisle, carefully examining paints, sketchbooks, and pencils.

Mia noticed the racks of fancy papers in all different prints. "I wonder if the paper is anything special."

"For the snowflakes?" Maddie asked.

Lulu held up a sheet of white paper covered with fine glitter. "This paper would be perfect for snowflakes!" It sparkled under the art store lights, and Mia had to agree.

"We should make some snowflakes!" Maddie said. "Just for fun. Could we, Miss Julia?"

"You can each choose two fancy pieces of paper," Miss Julia said. "And we'll buy three pairs of scissors too, since I didn't bring any with me on the plane."

After they made their purchases, they met Mom and Dad in the coffee shop. Miss Julia read the girls the first chapters of *From the Mixed-Up Files of Mrs. Basil E. Frankweiler* as Mom and Dad finished their cappuccinos.

"So, Claudia is running away with her little brother?" Lulu asked as Miss Julia closed the book.

"Yes, but remember, this is fiction," Miss Julia reminded them. "Just because kids in a story do something, that doesn't mean you should try it too, right?"

"It doesn't turn out all that great for Claudia and Jamie," Mia said. "Running away, I mean."

Maddie held up her hand. "Don't tell us what happens. I've never read this story."

Mia watched Mom and Dad take their final sips of cappuccino. "Is this one better?" She hoped so, because she didn't really want to traipse all over New York City visiting coffee shops.

"I'd say an 8.5," Dad said. "Good enough to give up the hunt for today."

The Glimmers and Miss Julia headed out of the coffee shop and onto the chilly sidewalk. Standing still for just a moment, Mom and Dad got their bearings, deciding which way to go and what to do.

"Tomorrow's a big day," Mom said. "We should grab a quick dinner and then go back to the hotel so you girls can get to sleep early."

"What about the map?" Lulu asked.

"We'll see if we have time," Mom said.

Dad stepped back into the shop and asked the barista about restaurants. As he steamed milk, the barista rattled off a few local places that were popular. Everyone agreed the noodle shop sounded delicious. As a result, they set out into the cold and walked the three blocks to the restaurant. Everyone ordered what sounded good to them, and they dove into their food. Mia especially liked the little tray of extras she could add to her noodles— crushed peanuts, fresh basil leaves, lime juice, and sweet and sour sauce.

After one last walk in the cold, they made their way back to the hotel. It was only six thirty, so Mom and Dad said they could do their Snow Angel research before going to sleep. Mia spread the map out on the bed.

Lulu uncapped the red pen. "Where should I mark?"

"Hold it!" Mia caught Lulu's hand. "We have to be sure before we mark anything."

"I know!" Lulu yanked her wrist away.

"We should call Ruby," Maddie reminded Mia, interrupting before a full-blown argument could erupt. "Before it gets too late."

"It's an hour earlier in Nashville," Miss Julia said. "But you're right, we should do it now while we're thinking about it."

Miss Julia dialed and handed her phone over to Maddie.

"It's ringing," Maddie said, and then shook her head. "Voice mail."

"Leave her a message," Mia said. "Maybe she'll want to watch tomorrow morning." As she said the words, her heart beat a little faster. Tomorrow morning, they'd be on television, and anyone could tune in and watch them live.

"Hey, Ruby," Maddie said. "Good news! Mia and I are going to be on the *Rise and Shine* show tomorrow with Mom—we get to talk about the Sparkle and Shine album! We wish you could be there with us, but we'll tell everyone about you and your idea. You should watch if you can. What time, Mom?" she called through to Mom and Dad's room.

"Nine a.m." Mom appeared in the doorway. "I'm not sure what segment of the show we'll be in, but *Rise and Shine* runs from nine to ten tomorrow morning."

"So does that mean it's at eight for Ruby?" Mia asked.

"Oh, that's right," Mom said. "Yes, the show is live."

"Sorry, Ruby," Maddie said, realizing she'd forgotten the voice mail was still recording. "Eight a.m. tomorrow morning on channel . . . ?"

"Four," Mom said.

"Four," Maddie told the phone. "Okay, well, talk to you later. Bye!"

She hung up and passed the phone back to Miss Julia.

"Okay, let's see where the Snow Angel has struck," Miss Julia said.

They'd just finished marking the last gift on the map when Mom said, "Lulu, it's time for you to go to bed."

"Don't Mia and Maddie need to go to bed too?" Lulu complained.

"They will soon," Mom said. "But I'd like to talk with them about tomorrow's interview, and I want you to get enough sleep so you're able to enjoy the show."

"I always have to go to bed first," Lulu complained. "I don't get to do anything."

Mia felt like pointing out that Lulu was actually getting her way, once again—sleeping on the rollaway. Or at least Mia was pretty sure that was the plan. Still, she'd rather stay up and talk with Mom and Dad about the interview than sleep on the rollaway.

"You got to go skating today," Mom reminded Lulu, kissing her on the top of her head. "And you did a double twirl, which I can't even do."

Lulu held tight to Mom's arm and dragged her into the girls' room. On her way out, Mom turned back. "Jack, maybe you can talk through possible questions with the girls. In case . . ."

She didn't need to explain in case of what. Lulu would obviously take forever going to bed. If Mia and Maddie were ever going to sleep tonight, they couldn't wait for Mom to talk them through the interview.

"Ready, girls?" Dad asked.

"Ready," they said, even though Maddie looked a little green. Now that *Rise and Shine* was just hours away, Mia had to admit that even she was feeling a little bit nervous. What if she froze and had no idea what to say?

NINE

All right, girls," Dad said. "Why don't you both sit there on the window seat and pretend it's a couch? You'll walk onstage with Mom and sit down. The host, Jennifer Jensen, will greet you."

"And we'll say hello," Mia said.

"Right. You okay, Maddie?" Dad asked.

Maddie was still a little green, but she nodded. "Yeah, I guess so. I was just picturing walking across the stage, and thinking about all the people in the audience and the cameras and everything. What if I trip?"

"You won't trip," Mia said.

"Plus, when you look out in the audience, you'll see me, Lulu, and Miss Julia. And if you don't look happy, we'll make faces at you until you smile," Dad teased.

"Oh, don't!" Maddie shook her head.

Dad's face lit up with a reassuring smile. "I promise, we won't do anything to distract you."

"And think of how fun it will be, Maddie," Mia said.

"I am excited to tell people about why we made the album," Maddie said.

"Right?" Mia nodded. "Think of how much more money we can raise with all those people hearing about it. How many people watch *Rise and Shine*, Dad?"

Maddie clapped her hands over her ears. "Don't answer that!"

Dad shook his head. "Won't say a word."

"So what questions do you think Jennifer will ask us?" Mia asked.

He ran them through a couple possible questions, letting them practice a few different answers. By the time they'd finished, Mom still hadn't returned, but Mia was starting to yawn. They had already picked out their outfits for the morning, so the girls slipped into their room and climbed under the covers. Mia was careful to lay her hair smoothly on her pillow so she wouldn't make any strange kinks in it while she slept. Mom stood up from where she'd been sitting beside Lulu's bed and kissed each of them good night. She left the door open when she went back to Dad.

" 'Night, Lulu," Maddie said.

" 'Night, Lulu," Mia echoed.

Lulu mumbled a half-hearted answer. Mia wished her sister could just be happy for them, rather than ruining the fun by being so upset. But, when she was honest with herself, she knew she wouldn't like it one bit if her sisters got to be on television and she didn't. Mia thought about how she felt watching Lulu on the ice with Mom and Dad. In school, kids talked about things being fair all the time. She and her sisters did too. But the truth was, in real life, it seemed like a lot of things weren't fair. No one said that sisters got to have the exact same experiences, she realized. But knowing that didn't make it any easier to be a sister.

She closed her eyes and waited to fall asleep. Her mind bounced from thought to thought, picturing tomorrow in a thousand different ways. She tried falling asleep in every way she could think to try. Finally, she realized the problem might be that she was trying to do this on her own. She took a deep breath, blew it out, and then began to silently pray. *God, I want to do a good job tomorrow. Maddie does too. Help us know what to say, so people understand why we made the album in the first place. And help all the teens who the album is for. Keep them safe tonight, wherever they are sleeping, which I'm sure isn't as warm and safe as where I'm sleeping. Thank you for all the gifts you give me and my family. In Jesus' name, Amen.*

After she prayed, she felt herself drifting off to sleep.

✳ ✳ ✳

"Wha . . . who?"

Mia felt Maddie thrashing around next to her. For a moment, she froze with fear, imagining all the things that might have gone wrong. Then she heard footsteps scurrying away, and Dad was there beside the bed and Mom was switching on the light.

"What's wro—" Mom's voice broke off, and she turned to look toward Lulu's rollaway.

Mia stared first at Maddie, then across at Lulu's empty bed, and then slowly reached up to finger her

hair. Sure enough, her hands came away sticky and stained—pink and blue and green. Maddie's hair was a mess of color too, as though someone had dumped a whole makeup box on her head—lipstick and blush and eye shadow. The lipstick was the worst because it made her hair clump and tangle. Mia was sure her head had to look just as bad. Her eyes filled with tears, as she pictured the way her hair had looked this afternoon, in Rhea's mirror. How could this have happened?

"Lulu!" Mom called, looking toward the bathroom, where a little patch of light spilled out from under the slightly ajar door.

Silence.

"Lulu, I know you're in there," Mom said. "Come on out."

Lulu did, finally, her hands stained with the same pink, blue, and green as Mia and Maddie's hair. Mia thought she didn't look nearly sorry enough.

"Lulu, why did you do this?" Maddie demanded, not waiting for Mom or Dad to ask.

"I . . ." Lulu looked around the room as though she might find the answer somewhere, and then burst into tears.

"She's only crying because she doesn't want to get in trouble," Mia said.

"Girls," Mom said, and the one word was enough to stop Mia in her tracks.

"Lulu, come with me." Dad held out his hand, and his serious face was worse than if he'd yelled. Lulu cried even harder as he carried her into the other room and closed the door.

Mia looked at her reflection and wailed, "What are we supposed to do about our hair? How could she do this?"

Mom held her arms out and pulled them both close, messy hair and all. "Let's wash out your hair, and then we can dry it again."

"But it won't be the same," Mia said.

"No," Mom said. "But we'll do our best. And after we all calm down a little, we can talk."

Mom brought in her special shampoo and conditioner and helped the girls scrub the mess out of their hair, while Dad talked with Lulu. Rather than drying their hair right away, Mom wrapped their heads in towels and they went to sit on the bed. Dad moved the rollaway into their room for the rest of the night, and then left Lulu so he could talk with Mia and Maddie.

"What did we ever do to her?" Mia demanded. Her anger felt like a cold, hard stone inside her chest.

"What Lulu did was very wrong," Mom said, making room on the bed for Dad. "Your hair is one thing, but what I'm even more concerned about are your hearts."

"It's absolutely understandable that you girls are angry, but if you let your anger turn into bitterness, it can take root and grow," Dad said. "And we don't want that, not for any of you."

Maddie stared down at her fingers, twisting and untwisting them. Mia could see the quiet storm brewing inside her and knew Maddie was stuffing her feelings down, trying to get control over them. Was that what they were supposed to do? Pretend they weren't angry?

"How are we supposed to forgive her?" Mia asked. "She ruins everything."

Dad shook his head sadly. "That's what I mean, Mia. If you tell yourself those kinds of things, you'll start believing them. And then you'll be on the watch for proof that you're right, that Lulu does ruin everything. Your bitterness will grow and grow, and it will eventually poison you."

"I don't feel like forgiving her," Maddie said, finally speaking up.

Mom took Maddie's hand in both of hers. "I'm sure you both need some time. But eventually, forgiveness will be a choice you can make."

"What about Lulu?" Mia asked, her anger flaring hot again. "Will she have to . . . I don't know . . . pay?"

"Absolutely, there will be consequences for her actions," Mom said.

"She won't be going to *Rise and Shine* tomorrow, to be in the studio audience," Dad said. "She'll stay here in the hotel with Miss Julia. Also, when we get back home, she'll have to do some extra chores to earn enough to replace Mom's makeup."

"Is that enough?" Mia grumbled.

"Is there any real way to pay for hurting you and Maddie like this?" Mom asked gently. "That's why our faith in Jesus is so important. We all do wrong things, and if we were required to pay for them on our own— fully—we'd never be able to do it."

"I still don't understand why she'd do this," Maddie said.

"Lulu isn't naughty just to be naughty," Mom said. "What she wants more than anything is to be big like you. Especially when you get special opportunities, like being invited to be on television."

"Tomorrow, we can discuss this more," Dad said. "It's important for you girls to talk about your frustrations. It's also important to try to see the situation from Lulu's perspective. I think we can all do that better after a good night's sleep."

"Will she have to see the situation from our perspective?" Mia asked.

"No one can force a person to be sorry, or to forgive," Mom said. "But both of those things are important, even if they are very, very difficult."

"I've asked Lulu to think about how it must feel to wake up and discover that your sister has done something like this. It will be important for you to talk with her about your feelings too, when you see her after your interview tomorrow," Dad said.

"I agree with Dad," Mom said. "We're all tired. How about you sleep with your hair wrapped in those towels? In the morning, Miss Julia and I will do our best to re-create your fancy hairdos. Okay?"

"Okay," Maddie said, her voice small and sad.

"Okay," Mia echoed.

"Good night," Mom said, tucking the covers under their chins.

"Sleep tight," Dad said, and kissed both girls on their foreheads.

It was a long time before Mia fell back asleep.

TEN

The morning was a flurry of hair-drying and getting dressed and bundling into the taxi to make it to the studio on time. Mia managed to entirely avoid Lulu, which was a relief. With all her nervous energy and her frustration over her hair not looking nearly as nice as it had yesterday, Mia was pretty sure she'd only make things worse by snapping at her sister.

"Girls, I'm so proud of you and your project," Mom said, as they sat in the studio's greenroom and waited for their cue. "You'll do wonderfully today, I know."

Fortunately, they didn't have to wait long. Soon they were swept backstage, and before Mia felt fully ready, it was time for their entrance. Dad was out in the studio audience, so even though Miss Julia and Lulu weren't there, the girls had a friendly face in the crowd. When they sat on the couch, Mia took Maddie's hand and squeezed it. Maddie didn't look as scared as Mia had expected her to look. The path to the couch had been completely clear, so neither she nor Maddie had tripped.

"Welcome," Jennifer Jensen said, beaming at Mia, Maddie, and Mom.

"Hello," Mom said.

Jennifer Jensen smiled out at the cameras. Next to the cameras, Mia saw text scrolling across a screen.

Jennifer managed to read the text, while also glancing at them and around at the audience. Mia tried to see if Jennifer said every word as written. It seemed as though Jennifer read the important parts but put some of the more casual conversation into her own words.

"Many of you know Gloria Glimmer," Jennifer was saying. "And these are two of her beautiful daughters, Mia and Maddie, who are here with news of their own. Let's start with you, though, Gloria. You're singing at the Light Up New York concert this Friday in Times Square."

"Yes," Mom said. "It's a joy to be part of the event, particularly this year when the city is dedicating the whole week to giving back to others."

"Yes, it is our first year to hold a citywide Light Up New York Week. Already, organizations and individuals across the city have launched projects aimed at giving back to the community." At this, Jennifer checked the screen for details. "We've had park clean-up crews, renovations of shelters across the city, and a Warm Hands, Warm Feet gloves and socks drive. A public art competition began yesterday, and artists in every corner of the city are exploring the theme of light in their chosen medium. Ceramic, paint, graffiti—the approved kind—fabric, music, and more. Street performance artists are even in on the fun. And, of course, our very own New York Snow Angel has upped the gift-giving campaign. It seems everywhere you turn, another mysterious gift has been left on a doorstep or park bench."

Light Up New York

At the mention of the Snow Angel, Mia glanced out into the audience at Dad, who winked back.

"So tell me, girls," Jennifer said, turning to Mia and Maddie. "You've made your first album—starting early! But it's not just any album. You recorded this album with a particular goal, correct?"

Mia could tell Maddie wanted her to answer this first question. She pressed her hands against her thighs and looked Jennifer in the eyes the way Dad had coached her. "That's right," she agreed. "Our friend Ruby, back home . . . She's watching, by the way. Hi, Ruby! Anyway, when Maddie and I met Ruby, we learned there are many reasons that a family might not have a home."

"Homelessness is difficult," Maddie chimed in. "For anyone. But for teenagers, it's especially lonely. And dangerous."

"That's why we decided to raise money with our album to help homeless teens," Mia said. "The album was Ruby's idea, actually. Maddie and I sing on it, with Ruby, and in one song our little sister, Lulu, even stars."

Mia hoped Lulu was watching back at the hotel. It was true that in Lulu's one song, she was the lead. Probably because she could never sing quietly. Also, she was the one who made the song work. Thinking about Lulu back at the hotel, Mia felt a tiny pang of sympathy. But she still didn't understand why her little sister had snuck around in the middle of the night and smeared their hair with makeup.

"Dad produced the album, and some of Mom's band members played for us," Maddie said. "Lots of people helped out with the project."

"Sounds like you have supporters who believe in your cause," Jennifer said. "Oh! I just had the best idea!"

Mia glanced at the screen to see if this was a scripted idea. Nope. Right now, the screen was blank.

"On Friday mornings, we air a short concert," Jennifer said, motioning to the stage. "We were going to use our own band this week, but now that you girls are in town, I wonder if you two might come and perform a song from your album?"

Mia looked at Maddie, who looked at Mom. Mom turned out to look at Dad, and Mia could see she felt put on the spot. Mia immediately knew why. What about Lulu? Everything was such a mess already. What would Lulu do if she didn't get to sing with them on Friday? Cut off their hair entirely in their sleep?

"We'd be so grateful," Jennifer said, filling the silence, which was becoming uncomfortable.

"Of course." Mom kept the hesitation out of her voice. "You'd like to perform, wouldn't you, girls?"

"Yes!" said Mia, and then nudged Maddie.

"Oh, yes," Maddie said, and even though Mia could tell her sister's enthusiasm was forced, she didn't think the audience would know.

"Well, we'll look forward to Friday, then," Jennifer said. "But before I let you go, we have a little surprise for you."

Another surprise? *What else?* Mia wondered.

"Thea Vance, a New York artist who specializes in glass, has created a line of snow globes for Light Up New York Week. Each one explores the theme of light and is a one of a kind," Jennifer said.

A crew member walked out from backstage, carrying a snow globe small enough to fit into the palm of her hand. Jennifer thanked her and held the snow globe up to catch the light. The cameras zoomed in, and everyone took in a collective breath. Mia and Maddie leaned in too.

Mia and her sisters loved snow globes. For Mia, it was something about the softness, the way the snow scrambled and then settled slowly, quietly, until it was left complete calm. Plus, looking at the scene inside the snow globe was like seeing a scene from a book come to life. The snow globe in Jennifer's hand glowed with an amber light, lit from inside by a lantern. A determined-looking girl held the lantern aloft. She held the reins of a sled pulled by six majestic white dogs—huskies or malamutes.

"Thea titled this snow globe 'Seeking Answers,'" Jennifer said. "And we'd like to give it to you, Mia and Maddie, as a thank you for all you're doing to help others."

Mia wasn't sure what to say. All those people watching. Such a beautiful gift.

"Thank you," Maddie breathed, finding her voice before Mia did.

"Yes, thank you," Mia echoed.

Jennifer seemed to glow a little too as she handed the snow globe to Maddie. "You're welcome, girls. And I encourage all our audience to check out Thea's line of snow globes. Proceeds from the sales support the arts in New York's schools."

The crowd cheered, and the cameras cut to commercials.

"Thank you so much for coming on the show," Jennifer said. "And I can't wait to see you on Friday, girls."

"Thank you for the beautiful gift," Mom said. "I know the girls will treasure it."

Jennifer gave each of them a hug, and then it was time to walk offstage. Maddie almost tripped on the way out. Both she and Mia dove to protect the snow globe. Once they were sure it was safe, they burst into giggles. Good thing the camera hadn't filmed them on the way out.

ELEVEN

As soon as they came out the stage door, Dad scooped them up in a giant hug. "You were wonderful, girls!"

They hugged him back, and then showed him the snow globe as they waited for a taxi to take them to the hotel.

On the cab ride back to the hotel, Mia and Maddie studied the snow globe, noticing all the tiny details. The snow globe scene had a little magic to it, magic Mia hadn't seen from a distance when Jennifer had first shown it to them. For one thing, the girl wasn't headed toward just any forest. Purple and peacock-blue trees filled the forest, their curlicued branches filled with miniature dots of light. The lights looked like fireflies among their metallic gold and silver leaves.

"I'm not sure we should show Lulu the snow globe," Mia said to Maddie.

Maddie bit her lip. "But, Mia, I'm sure she watched the show. She'll know about it."

"Mom, could you maybe put it away somewhere safe?" Mia asked. "So she doesn't break it or anything?"

"I understand that you're not on the best terms with Lulu right now. But I don't think Lulu would break your snow globe on purpose," Mom said.

"But she might on accident," Mia pressed. "Or maybe she actually would break it on purpose. You know she'll be mad about the concert now, and when she's mad, look what she does."

"Lulu smeared our hair with makeup in the middle of the night," Maddie spoke up. "Mia's right. I love Lulu, and I know I will forgive her for what happened last night, but how are we supposed to trust her?"

"You know, Maddie, you're right," Mom said, nodding. "I love you girls so much that I want to instantly make everything all right. Broken trust hurts, and I don't want any of my beautiful girls to be in pain. But it's true. Forgiveness is a choice, one we can—and should—make right away. Restoring trust, on the other hand, does take time."

Mia considered the unkind thoughts that so often came to mind when she thought about Lulu. "How do you know if you've honestly forgiven someone? I mean, if you don't trust them yet?"

"It's important to understand that forgiveness isn't a feeling," Dad said. "Like Mom said, it's a firm decision that we make, one we don't allow to change based on our feelings. But after we've made the choice to forgive, we need God's help."

"You girls always inspire me with the way you pray," Mom said. "And I encourage you to pray for God to help soften your hearts toward Lulu. But it will also help if you pray for Lulu too. If you pray for God to bless

Lulu, that will help fix what's broken between you. It may take some time for things to feel right between you, and if it does, that's completely normal."

When they walked into the hotel room, Lulu bounded over. She gave Mia and Maddie each a hug, pressing envelopes into their hands.

"I'm really, really sorry," Lulu said, her eyes brimming with tears.

Mia didn't know what to say and was grateful for the envelope, which gave her a reason to walk away, sit down, and take a moment. She slipped the note out of the envelope, not expecting very much. Of course, Lulu would say she was sorry. She'd want everything to be back to normal. But how were she and Maddie supposed to know whether Lulu was sorry enough not to do something like it again? She took a minute to read the note.

> Dear Mia,
> I was only thinking about me and not about you when I put makeup in your hair. I'm sorry. I really, really am. Will you forgive me?
> Love, Lulu

The ink around the words *only* and *Lulu* had smeared—Mia was pretty sure these were tearstains. Maybe saying sorry wasn't enough, but it did seem like Lulu really meant the words in her letter. Mia folded the note and slipped it back into the envelope, thinking about what Mom and Dad had said last night about honestly telling Lulu how they felt.

"It made me really angry, waking up and finding out that our hair was ruined," Mia said quietly to Lulu.

Maddie nodded, but didn't go so far as to say that she was angry too. Mia knew that her sister hated conflict, and that putting her feelings into words might be more than she could do right now.

Tears rolled down Lulu's cheeks, but she wasn't wailing and putting on a show like she sometimes did. She just looked truly and honestly sorry. Mia thought about what Mom and Dad had said earlier, in the cab, about forgiveness being a choice. She couldn't pretend that everything was all right, or that she completely trusted Lulu now, just because of her note and her tears. But she could choose to forgive her.

Mia crossed the room and pulled Lulu into a hug. "I forgive you, Lulu."

As she said the words, she prayed, *God, help me stick to this decision.*

"I do too," Maddie said, joining the hug.

"We watched you on television," Miss Julia said, smiling at the three sisters.

"You're going to sing on Friday," Lulu said, smiling bravely.

"That invitation was such a surprise," Mom said. "I'm sorry that you aren't included, Lulu."

"It's okay," Lulu said, but Mia knew it wasn't.

If Lulu wasn't complaining about the concert, she must honestly feel sorry about what she'd done to their hair. Looking at Lulu's too-bright eyes and knowing how hard her little sister was working to have a good attitude, Mia's frustration cracked open, just a little.

"Come see our snow globe." Mia sat on Mom and Dad's bed and held it out for Lulu to see.

Lulu looked without touching, and then she asked, "Can I shake it?"

Mia scooted into the center of the bed. She motioned for Lulu to join her, so that if the snow globe fell, the mattress would break its fall.

Lulu shook the snow globe gently, and then held it in the palm of her hand while the glitter swirled and settled.

"It's a fairy forest!" Lulu said.

Maddie gasped with a sudden idea and clapped her hands. "We should make up a story about it, Lulu."

"Together?" Lulu asked, looking surprised.

"Sure," Maddie said. "But you can start it, since you're the fairy expert."

"Okay," Lulu said. "I'll have to think about it."

"For now," Mom said, "let's put this treasure away and get ready for the day's adventure."

Mom closed the snow globe in the drawer next to her bed, and Mia hoped that would be safe enough.

"You said we could go to a toy store today," she reminded Mom and Dad. "And the library."

Lulu's eyes became a little watery again. "Do I have to stay home all day?"

"No," Mom said. "I think you're ready to join us, and our Glimmer family adventure wouldn't be the same without you."

Miss Julia checked the directions on her phone. "The library is just down the street, and the toy store is a few blocks in the opposite direction."

"I think we should walk then," Dad said. "And we can find some lunch along the way too."

Miss Julia helped the girls gather their coats, gloves, and hats, and soon everyone was bundled up and ready to go on the next adventure.

"Wait!" Mia said, as they were just about to leave the rooms. "We should take our Snow Angel map, just in case."

"Good idea!" Maddie agreed. "We might pass one of the Snow Angel sites. You never know, there might be clues."

Outside the hotel, the streets were as busy as ever. Other families passed by, arms full of shopping bags. Lots of people hurried past, looking like they were out on their lunch breaks.

"Can we go to the toy store first?" Mia asked.

Dad quirked an eyebrow. "I don't know, I'm pretty hungry."

"Please?" Maddie asked.

"With a cherry on top?" Lulu asked, a little of her bounce starting to come back.

As they turned the corner, there was the toy store. Whirligigs, dolls, and toys of every kind filled the brightly lit windows on either side of the red door. Above the door, a sign read, *Mr. Thabbet's Baubles and Trinkets.*

"What's a bau-ble?" Lulu asked, sounding the unfamiliar word out.

"Baubles are like trinkets," Miss Julia said, and then looked the word up on her phone. "The dictionary says that 'baubles are small, showy trinkets.'"

"And trinkets are little things that aren't all that important, right?" Maddie asked.

"Toys are important!" Lulu insisted.

"They seem to be," Dad agreed. "Considering the number of toys we dragged along with us on this trip."

"Dad!" the girls all chimed together.

He grinned and reached into his pocket, handing them each a crisp bill. "Ten dollars for each of you. You can use your money as you choose. But once the ten dollars are gone, they're gone."

"Yay!" Lulu cheered. "Thank you, Daddy!"

"Thank you!" Mia and Maddie agreed.

TWELVE

When they opened the little red door, a cheerful bell tinkled. The girls hurried inside, darting from one shelf to another. Mia scanned the bookshelves, and then something on a shelf nearby caught her eye. It was a detective kit, complete with a magnifying glass, a notepad, and a tiny pen for jotting down clues on the go. The kit also included rearview glasses with mirrors that showed what was happening behind you. She checked the price tag and sighed. $15.99. So much for that. But as she continued walking around the store, she thought about Lulu's bright eyes, and how hard Lulu was trying to have a good attitude. She also thought about what Mom had said last night about Lulu wanting to be like them, to be included.

Lulu was busy looking at the stuffed animals, so Mia quietly took Maddie's arm. "Come here."

"What?" Maddie asked, as Mia brought her over to the little table.

"What if we bought Lulu a detective kit?" Mia asked. "I can't do it myself, because it's $15.99. But we could do it together. I really don't want our whole trip to New York to feel like a giant fight. Maybe if we included her in solving the mystery, she wouldn't feel so left out. What do you think?"

Maddie nodded slowly, the idea catching on with her. She broke into a smile. "Yes! I think she'll love it!"

Mia and Maddie checked to make sure Lulu was still distracted with the stuffed animals. She was, so they bought the kit. The clerk filled the bright red bag with red-and-white-polka-dot tissue paper.

"What's that?" Lulu asked, arriving at the counter with her chosen animal, a beanbag ladybug big enough to be a miniature pillow.

"You'll see," Mia said.

Mia and Maddie couldn't even wait until they were out of the store. They were so excited to give Lulu her gift that they handed her the bag and stepped back a little, with Mom, Dad, and Miss Julia watching from the side.

"For me?" she asked, eyes wide.

"For you!" they said.

As soon as she saw the kit, Lulu sat right down on the toy store floor and took out all the pieces. She put the pad and pen in her pocket and tried on the rearview glasses. "Whoa!" she said.

"How about you try looking for clues on our way to lunch?" Dad suggested.

Lulu packed her kit up. Leaving the glasses on, she tried out a new spy walk as she slipped out the door with Miss Julia and Dad.

Mom wrapped her arms around Mia and Maddie. "I'm proud of you, girls."

All through lunch, Lulu spied on people at the tables behind them, reporting back to Mia and Maddie. She started counting times a teenage girl stole looks at her cell phone, which her mom kept telling her to put away. "Fifty-two!" Lulu said, about halfway through her sandwich. Mia was impressed that Lulu had watched long enough to count fifty-two glances.

They thought about taking their shopping bags back to the hotel, but in the end, they decided to go straight to the library, since it was now on their way. They pulled on hats and gloves again before going outside. Light snowflakes had started to fall. They crossed the street and headed up the block toward the library.

"Do you think people will still sleep outside on Friday night, even if it's snowing?" Maddie asked.

"I think so," Dad said. "Even if it's not snowing, everyone knew this event would be during a cold time of year."

"It's hard to believe that some people sleep outside every night, whether it's cold and snowing, or raining or whatever," Maddie said.

"I agree," Mom said. "That's one reason I'm so proud to be part of the event on Friday, and so proud of what you girls are doing too, with the Sparkle and Shine album."

"Look, a reporter!" Mia pointed the camera crew out to Maddie and Lulu. "I'll bet it's the Snow Angel again!"

"Hold on there." Dad stopped the girls from charging ahead to see. "Let's go together, just in case."

"Wouldn't it be wonderful if every urgent news story was about the Snow Angel?" Mom asked.

"We have to see if there are any clues!" Lulu took off her glasses and fished the magnifying glass out of her bag. If Miss Julia hadn't caught Lulu's hand, Mia was sure she would have charged down the sidewalk ahead of everyone.

As it was, Lulu dragged Miss Julia all the way to the steps of the New York Public Library. Two stone lions peered out over the crowd that had collected to watch the reporter and camera crew. Everyone had to scramble to keep up. In a way, Mia was happy that Lulu was so excited about the detective kit. Maybe the kit would help Lulu feel more included. Maybe then she'd stop focusing on making her sisters' lives miserable. Well, Mia knew her little sister didn't mean to make life miserable, but it wasn't easy always being on edge, not knowing what bad thing would happen next. *God, I've chosen to forgive her*, Mia prayed. *Help me have a good attitude.*

When they were close enough to see the reporter's hands, they saw that she was, in fact, holding a paper snowflake. She said, "And that's it for this newest Snow Angel delivery. We hope that soon we'll learn his or her identity and be able to thank this giver of gifts properly."

The camera's light turned off, and the crowd began to disperse.

"Wait, what was the gift?" Maddie asked, as people streamed by.

"A pair of reading glasses on a beaded chain," a woman stopped to say. "For one of the tour guides here at the library who is always losing her glasses. Such an odd giver, this Snow Angel is. No rhyme or reason to the gifts, no way to predict what's coming next."

"Should we look for footprints?" Lulu asked, taking out her magnifying glass. She covered one eye and peered through the glass with her other one, nearly running into someone coming down the steps.

"Lulu, how can you even tell whose footprints you're looking at?" Mia asked before she could stop herself. She wanted Lulu to be excited about clues. But seriously. At least forty people had just come down these stairs, and how many more might have been here since the Snow Angel had passed by? How would anything that Lulu found in the muddy snow be worth anything?

"What if we take a tour with the guide who was given the glasses?" Maddie suggested. "Maybe we can even ask her some questions about who has been on her tour recently. She might have ideas."

Lulu gazed at Maddie through her magnifying glass. Through the thick glass, her eye was large and round, making both Mia and Maddie giggle. Lulu grinned too, and then put the glass away, taking out her detective pad and pen. "Let's do it. I'll take notes."

"So, into the library?" Dad pulled Mom close.

She shivered and leaned into him, making Mia realize how cold her own cheeks and nose were. It would be nice to go inside and warm up, even if they didn't find any Snow Angel clues. But Mia thought Maddie might be on to something. If the tour guide noticed something major, she probably would have told the reporters. But sometimes it took the just-right question for someone to realize she had seen something important. Mia had learned this from the mysteries she and her sisters had solved so far this year.

"Into the library!" Maddie said, and led the way.

THIRTEEN

The library wasn't like any Mia had ever seen before. In fact, it looked more like a cathedral or a museum. For one thing, she couldn't see a single book when she came through the front doors. Two grand staircases stood on each side of the entryway, over which hung wrought iron light fixtures. Marble candelabras stood watchfully next to archways, casting warm light across the entire space. People crisscrossed the room, headed upstairs or toward the gift shop, or along the hallway that stretched behind the entryway. Off to their left was a welcome desk.

They might have stood there staring around the room for a while, if Miss Julia hadn't noticed the welcome desk had a sign that read *Tours* hanging above it.

"We don't have a tour for another 45 minutes." The woman behind the desk took off her reading glasses and let them hang around her neck on their beaded chain. "While you wait, you could watch the 30-minute film on the making of the library. Then you'll be experts when you go on the tour. You'll know what to look for."

"Are those glasses from the Snow Angel?" Lulu asked, not beating around the bush.

"Lulu," Mia warned.

"What? We're looking for clues, aren't we?" Lulu asked.

"You're looking for clues?" the woman asked.

"The Snow Angel has captivated the girls," Dad explained.

"Have you found any clues yet?" the woman wanted to know.

"No, but we just started looking," Mia said. "I'm Mia, and that's Maddie, and Lulu. And our Mom and Dad, Jack and Gloria Glimmer, and our nanny, Miss Julia."

Mia hoped that if she introduced the family, the woman would introduce herself too. And maybe tell them anything else she knew.

"Well, hello," the woman said. "I'm Diane Jackson, and as you have suspected, I did have a visit from the Snow Angel. Unfortunately, I don't believe I have any more information for you. I suppose the Snow Angel would have to be someone observant, someone who noticed that I lost my glasses at some point or another. But I lose my glasses almost every day, so it's not easy to pin down when someone might have noticed."

"Has anyone been on your tour more than once, recently?" Maddie asked. "Maybe someone who seemed particularly interested or who asked a lot of questions?"

Mia was impressed with Maddie's questions. She was right. If the Snow Angel was specifically watching the librarian, he or she may have taken the tour more than once. Or, at least, the Snow Angel would have taken an interest and asked questions.

Diane frowned, thinking. "You know, other than a family with a couple little girls who came two weeks in a row, I can't think of anyone who has taken the tour twice recently. But it wasn't all that unusual for that family to take two tours, because they took different ones. In one, they saw the whole library, and in the other they explored the map room in depth. The parents mentioned they were trying out indoor adventures for the winter, since it's been so cold. Their girls seemed interested, but in a good way. Like kids who don't spend too much time staring at screens." She cocked her head at Mom and Dad, and then raised her eyebrows at the girls. "I suppose they were a little like you girls. But none of you are the Snow Angel, are you?"

Maddie and Lulu laughed, shaking their heads. Mia smiled too, but she didn't like the realization that the Snow Angel could be anyone. Anyone in the entire city of New York . . . and that was a lot of people. Had she and her sisters finally taken on an impossible-to-solve mystery?

"How many people live in New York?" Mia asked Miss Julia, as they settled into the cushy chairs in the small movie-screening room. She couldn't remember what Miss Julia had said on the first day they were in town.

Miss Julia took out her phone. After tapping and scrolling, she said, "Eight point four six million, and that was back in 2013. Also, on average, there are 538,000 tourists in the city every day."

Mia flopped her head against the cushioned headrest.

"We're going to find the Snow Angel," Lulu said, patting Mia's arm. "Don't worry. I'm sure we will."

Mia wasn't so sure.

"Remember, you promised to have fun even if you couldn't solve the mystery," Mom said as the lights dimmed. "Right now, let's enjoy the library, okay?"

Mia hadn't expected the library movie to be interesting, but before she knew it, she was completely absorbed. The movie showed the history of the library's construction and its opening in 1911, and gave quick peeks into different rooms. Each held special collections like rare books, old manuscripts, and even a photography collection. Mia kept track of what she wanted to see—the reading rooms, the children's book room, of course, and the map room.

"What do you think, should we go on the actual tour?" Dad asked.

"I think we can just wander on our own," Mom said. "Now that we know so much about the different rooms."

The girls agreed, since they'd already had a chance to talk to Diane. For the next hour or so, they popped in and out of the galleries, looking at the statues and paintings all over the building. Even though he'd already given them a treat at the toy store, Dad offered to buy the girls each a book in the gift shop. Mia was pretty sure this was because she and Maddie had used their money on Lulu. Mia chose *When You Reach Me*, which was a Newbery Award book set in New York, and Maddie chose a sketchbook full of ideas called *642 Things to Draw*. Lulu chose a picture book called *Library Lion*. In the movie, they'd learned the names of the marble lions outside—Patience and Fortitude. Now, Lulu was obsessed with the idea that the lions came to life at night.

"I'm sorry we didn't find any clues," Maddie said to Mia as they left the library.

"I didn't think about there being so many people in New York, or so many possibilities," Mia said. "And we can keep looking, anyway. It's still fun looking for clues, even if we don't figure the mystery out."

"I was starting to think we could solve any mystery," Maddie said.

Mia looped her arm through Maddie's. "Yeah, me too."

Lulu posed with each of the lions in front of the library building, and Miss Julia snapped photos. Then, she took a full family photo in front of the library and checked her watch.

"I have to catch my train to Brooklyn soon," she said.

"Where are you going?" Mia asked.

"To see a friend. We're meeting for dinner," Miss Julia said.

"And I have a surprise planned for the rest of us tonight," Dad said, and then clamped his mouth shut, refusing to say anything more.

For the rest of the walk home, the only mystery anyone tried to solve was the surprise Dad had up his sleeve.

FOURTEEN

Mom had packed fancy dresses for the girls, which they decided to wear tonight. Dad refused to tell anyone—even Mom—where they were going.

"It's a surprise," he kept saying.

While Mia, Maddie, and Lulu waited for the adults to finish getting ready, the girls sat with the snow globe, passing it back and forth and telling stories about the girl and what she found in the magical woods. "It's like Narnia," Maddie insisted. "With talking animals . . ."

"And fairies!" Lulu put in.

"But she's seeking answers," Mia pointed out. "So, maybe she's trying to solve a mystery."

For now, though, Mia didn't want to think about the Snow Angel mystery. Every time she thought about the mystery, it felt like she was mentally grasping for threads, each thought breaking off soon after it began. All that broken-end thinking made her head hurt.

Dad popped his head in the doorway. "Are you girls ready?"

He was wearing a dark suit, and Mom wore a sparkly dress and heels. Excitement fizzed through Mia as she considered all the possible surprises. Mom put the snow globe away in the drawer, and then they were off.

Down the elevator and into the lobby, the Glimmers went. Through glass double doors, they found a little underground hallway that led to Grand Central Terminal.

"It's like a secret passageway," Maddie said, delighted.

Mia loved this idea. She imagined that they were entering a train station that not only transported people all over the city, but to impossible places. Like forward and back in time. Or into magical worlds, like inside the snow globe.

At first, the station felt more like an underground mall with its rows of shops. Soon, they stepped into a wide open area. Mia stopped, staring. How could something this big be tucked away, nearly underneath their hotel? The cavernous space reminded her of the library. Like the library, it felt both cold because of all the stone, and warm because of the color of the lights shining against the walls and ceiling. Overhead, painted constellations adorned a deep green, arched ceiling.

"Welcome to Grand Central, girls," Dad said, navigating through the crowd to steps and up onto a balcony. Right there, in the middle of the station, under that giant, beautiful ceiling, was a restaurant filled with elegant tables covered in white cloths. The waiter led them to a table that overlooked the station. Mia watched people come and go. Any one of them could be the Snow Angel on his or her way to give a gift.

"You know who I think the Snow Angel is?" Lulu asked no one in particular.

Lulu had put on her rearview glasses and had her back to the balcony so she could watch the people below without looking at them.

"Who?" Mia scanned the crowd, assuming Lulu had chosen someone random to suspect.

"I think it's someone famous. Like Taylor Swift or someone."

"Why do you think so?" Maddie asked, taking this idea seriously.

Mia realized this actually wasn't a bad theory.

Lulu shrugged. "Well, famous people are the ones who want to be invisible sometimes, right? Like that person down there wearing the giant sunglasses inside when she doesn't have to. She could be famous, right?"

Mia leaned forward, straining to see. "Where?"

"She's already gone," Lulu said.

"You're wearing giant sunglasses," Mia pointed out.

"Because I'm a detective." Lulu adjusted her glasses and angled her neck to check the view again.

"It could be someone famous," Maddie said. "There are a lot of famous people who live in New York, right?"

"True . . ." Mom said.

"Would you do something in secret like that, Mom?" Maddie asked.

"I'd have to think about it," Mom said. "Right now, it seems like the mystery is drawing more attention to gift-giving, and that's a good thing. I mean, there are so many people who need things and cannot or would not get them themselves for one reason or another. But I find that if I talk about a cause, the way you girls are doing with your album, I can help point attention toward the issues I think are important. Then my hope is that people want to join in."

"I want to be a Snow Angel," Lulu said.

Dad plucked the spyglasses off her nose. "Right now, what you need to do is decide what you want to eat. We have to order, because another surprise is coming."

"Another surprise?" Mia asked.

"What is it, what is it?" Lulu asked, completely distracted from the clue-seeking.

Dad handed her the menu. "Let's start with what you want to eat."

All the girls ordered cheesy pasta and fancy fizzy drinks in their favorite flavors. Mia chose passionfruit, and her glass came topped with a slice of pineapple and a raspberry. Maddie chose strawberry, and Lulu chose pineapple. Both of their drinks came with fruit skewers on top too. When everyone finished eating, they bundled up and headed up the rest of the station's steps and out onto the sidewalk.

"Where are we going?" Lulu asked.

Mom raised her eyebrows, smiling a hopeful smile. "I have an idea."

"Do you?" Dad teased.

Light Up New York

When they arrived at the theater a few blocks later, Mia wondered how she hadn't guessed. They'd walked past this theater a few times in the past couple days. She'd seen the sign for *Peter Pan*, but she hadn't thought they'd get to go to the show. Dad had bought seats near the stage.

"A Broadway show!" Lulu said, flinging her arms wide, as though she was seeing her own name in lights.

Dad laughed, clearly delighted that the girls liked the surprise. "Come sit down, Lulu. Technically, this is off-Broadway. But, you're right. New York City is one of the best places in the world to see theater."

"What makes it off-Broadway?" Mia asked.

"A few things," Dad said. "But the main way that they distinguish between Broadway and off-Broadway in New York is that if a production is put on in a theater with five hundred seats or more, it's a Broadway show. Theaters with more than one hundred seats and less than five hundred are off-Broadway."

"And what if there are less than one hundred seats?" Lulu asked.

"Then, it's an off-off-Broadway show," Mom explained.

"Since it's *Peter Pan*, will the actors fly?" Maddie asked.

Her question was answered soon after the lights went down. When Peter showed up at the Darling house, he flew from backstage through the open window, and then straight out over the audience. As Peter's feet skimmed near their heads, Mia gasped. She knew that Peter must be flying using some kind of rope, but she couldn't see a thing, even when he had come so close.

Mia let herself be swept into the story. She imagined herself up on stage, dancing, singing, flying. What would it feel like to fly over the heads of the audience like that?

At intermission, Maddie caught Mia's arm before they stood up to go into the lobby. "Those invisible wires make me keep thinking about the Snow Angel. Do you think he's staying hidden with some kind of trick?"

"If so, I have no idea what the trick would be," Mia said. "It's the most un-mystery kind of mystery ever. There aren't any clues. There aren't any red herrings. There isn't anything but a bunch of questions."

"Well, the mystery is keeping Lulu happy, anyway." Maddie nodded at Lulu, who was back to wearing her rearview glasses and spying on the people in the row behind them.

"True," Mia agreed.

"So what do you think of the show, girls?" Mom asked.

"It's amazing," Mia said.

"Exactly," Maddie agreed.

"Good surprise?" Dad asked.

"Great surprise," the girls agreed.

FIFTEEN

reakfast in bed!" Lulu crowed the next morning, as Dad brought in trays of eggs and pancakes with maple syrup.

They'd gotten in late from the show the night before and fallen into bed so exhausted, they hadn't even had time to fight over what to watch on television while they fell asleep. Now, Lulu was already out of bed and dancing around the room.

"Today, we don't have any commitments." Mom dodged a wild swing of Lulu's arm, narrowly missing spilling her pitcher of orange juice. "So, we can explore the city. I thought we could take a double-decker bus to see some of the most important and famous sights, and then we can ride in a boat to see the Statue of Liberty."

"A boat?" Mia asked.

"The statue faces out toward the ocean, so the best way to get to her is by boat." Dad handed a tray to Mia and Maddie. "Then the boat will take us right up to Liberty Island, where we can get out and see the statue up close."

"Can we also see the Metropolitan Museum of Art today?" Mia asked.

"I was thinking we should go tomorrow," Mom said.

"That's good, because we still need to make up our scavenger hunt," Maddie said. "We've barely had time to read *From the Mixed-Up Files* with Miss Julia."

"True, we haven't even made it to the part that takes place in the museum," Mia said. "But it won't spoil the book to look for the places even if you haven't read about them yet."

"Lulu, come have some breakfast," Dad said, setting her tray on the rollaway bed.

Mia realized that Lulu was now dancing with the snow globe in her hand, shaking the snow with each cha-cha-cha. "Lulu! Put that down!"

"I wasn't going to break it," Lulu said defensively.

"Mia and Lulu," Mom warned.

Mia knew she shouldn't have snapped—but she hadn't been able to stop herself. The snow globe was supposed to be safe in Mom's drawer. Look how easily Lulu had gotten it and started messing around with it.

"We know you wouldn't ever mean to break it," Maddie said, using the calm voice she often did when she tried to avoid a fight between her sisters. "But we also know that accidents happen all the time, and we don't want the special snow globe smashed or anything," she tried to explain.

Lulu set the snow globe down on the bedside table with a little thump. "I don't break things!"

Mia flinched, halfway expecting to hear the shatter of glass.

"How about we start the morning over again?" Dad said. "Lulu, why don't you climb back into bed and we can start with breakfast in bed."

"Okay," Lulu mumbled, climbing back into bed.

Mom took the snow globe back to her room to put it away in the drawer. Even though pancakes were one of Lulu's favorites—especially drowned in maple syrup—Lulu only picked at her food. Mia felt bad for having snapped at her, but if Lulu broke the snow globe, there wouldn't be any un-breaking it. Especially since it was one of a kind. Lulu traded her fork for the remote and clicked on the television. She started flipping through channels.

"I don't think we need to watch—" Mom began.

"Wait, go back!" Maddie said. "It's about the Snow Angel!"

"Can we just watch this?" Mia asked. "In case there are clues?"

Mom shook her head at Dad, but didn't say no.

"Turn it up please, Lulu!" Mia said, leaning forward to listen.

A map of New York, much like the one the girls had labeled, lit up the wall behind the anchorwoman. She pointed out various sites where gifts had been left, reminding everyone of the wide range the Snow Angel had covered.

"Gifts have been given to the old, the young, and everyone in between. The Snow Angel doesn't only choose the homeless or the very poor as recipients, but also others who may be overlooked for one reason or another. Every gift has a story. Every recipient has a need. And the question remains . . . how can the Snow Angel possibly know each of these people, their needs, and their stories?"

The anchorwoman gestured to the map. "We've had another gift today. It was a pair of thick wool socks, left next to the first stop of the Red Line tour bus, along with the signature snowflake. The card was addressed to Ruthie, one of the tour guides, with the note: "For your cold toes on windy days."

The cameras cut to Ruthie and the on-the-spot reporter. "Why do you think the Snow Angel left you socks?"

"Well, on cold days, I often forget my extra pair. Wind whips up that stairwell on the tour bus and freezes my toes."

The reporter's eyes lit up. "Which day did you forget your socks? Did you mention your cold feet on one of your recent tours?"

Ruthie laughed. "Just about every other day, sweetheart."

Disappointment flashed across the reporter's face. Mia knew she'd hoped that somehow the new gift might lead to a clue—any clue—about who the Snow Angel might be.

"Wait!" Mia jumped off the bed, excited by a sudden idea. "That tour bus, couldn't we try to take it? We could meet Ruthie and ask her questions. We could finally find our first clue!"

"Wait, Mia . . ." Maddie bit her lip, worried. "Remember what happened at the library? Won't Ruthie just say that she has no idea, like Diane did?"

"But what if she says something about a family with two parents and two little girls?" Mia asked. "Then, it would be a pattern."

"The Snow Angel isn't two parents and two girls," Lulu said. "It can't be."

"It could be anyone," Mia said. "All I'm saying is that the more people we talk to who received gifts from the Snow Angel, the better. Even if they didn't know they saw anything special, we know the Snow Angel must have been close to them at some point. Maybe when we compare what they say, something will come clear."

Maddie raised an eyebrow. "Like maybe Ruthie the tour guide saw someone famous on her tour."

"Right," Mia said. "Then, we could go back and ask Diane if she'd seen that same person."

"Or at least someone in sunglasses!" Lulu said, up on her feet, bouncing on the bed, now swept up in this idea.

"Wait, wait, wait," Dad said, holding up his hands. "Girls, there are at least three different bus tour companies in the city, and each company has more than one bus. How could we possibly be sure we got onto Ruthie's tour?"

"Oh," Mia said, feeling the excitement dissolve out of her.

"Well, maybe we could find her," Lulu said, "if I wear my rearview glasses."

Mia had to smile. "Maybe that will work, Lulu."

"I think the bus on the news was red," Maddie said. "Like the buses in London. And I am sure buses from other companies are different colors, wouldn't you say?"

"Yes, I think so," Dad slowly answered.

"Well, at least we can look for a red bus," Maddie said. "And we can even ask if the people on the bus know Ruthie. Maybe it isn't as hard as it seems."

"As long as you understand we're not promising to traipse all over the city looking for one specific tour guide," Dad said. "After all, we have a whole city to see!"

"Can we go now?" Mia asked.

Mom looked over their plates. "Two more bites, and then we'll get ready."

Mia took her two bites, and then scrambled out of bed to choose clothes. She had a good feeling about today. Maybe today would be the day they'd finally find a clue.

SIXTEEN

Dad checked with the concierge at the hotel and confirmed that tour buses usually took off from Times Square.

"Just head on up 42nd a few blocks, and you can catch a bus there." The concierge handed Dad a map.

"Look!" Maddie said, pointing out the photo of the bus on their map. "It's a red bus!"

Mia nodded, hopeful. Just because they hadn't found any clues so far didn't mean they wouldn't today.

Miss Julia passed out hats, gloves, and scarves, and everyone bundled up before heading out. Miss Julia had even tucked a couple blankets in her oversized bag, just in case they needed extra warmth on the bus and boat rides. Outside, it was snowing a little more steadily than it had yesterday. Lulu made a game of holding out her tongue, trying to catch snowflakes in her mouth. There wasn't enough snow to gather on the ground, but a light ghosting of flakes skittered here and there across the sidewalk. Soon, they made their way to Times Square.

"Do you think it's too cold for a bus tour?" Mom wondered aloud.

"Maybe we should bring some hot chocolate along," Dad suggested.

Mia could see him starting to scheme. "You mean coffee?" she teased Dad a little.

"Well, if the hot chocolate shop happened to have coffee, I wouldn't complain," Dad said.

So, Miss Julia looked up the best coffee shops within walking distance. Fortunately, there was one with five stars just down the block. So the Glimmers walked down the street to the shop and ordered warm drinks for everyone. Mia liked the way the warmth from the liquid radiated from her cup, warming her fingers inside her gloves. Soon, they were back on the street, looking for the red tour bus.

"Over there!" Maddie said, spotting one.

They crossed the street and found the man selling tickets underneath the tour bus sign.

"Which tour is Ruthie's?" Lulu asked.

The man laughed, pulling out his envelope of tickets and counting out six tickets for them. "She's a popular one today. But, I'm sure there's room on her tour if you're willing to wait. She's up next . . . The bus should be here in about twenty minutes."

"We might need more coffee, then," Dad said.

"Dad!" the girls said, all groaning a little.

"Let's poke inside a few shops," Mom said. "To keep warm until it's time to go."

After Dad paid for the tickets, the family wandered in and out of a few clothing stores. Finally, a red bus pulled up.

"Come on, come on!" Lulu urged.

In the end, there was plenty of room for the Glimmers and Miss Julia, especially because they wanted to sit in the top section of the bus. They introduced themselves to Ruthie, and then chose seats at the front of the bus. Ruthie stood in the stairwell, a few rows back, but it was easy to turn around and see her. As passengers boarded, Ruthie greeted each one. Mia could see why the Snow Angel had liked Ruthie. Like Diane from the library, Ruthie was energetic and welcoming, the kind of person who made you feel like a friend the minute you met her.

"We can see everything from here!" Mia said.

"And everyone," Lulu stage whispered, putting on her rearview glasses. Now she could watch Ruthie without turning around.

"And everyone," Mia agreed.

"You should wear the headphones," Ruthie said to the Glimmers, motioning to the cords plugged into the bus wall. "Makes it easier to hear me when we start driving."

There were three sets of headphones per seat, with cords long enough to reach the headphone jack in the wall even if you sat in the aisle seat. The girls worked on untangling their cords and plugging in, and then Miss Julia passed out blankets so everyone could cover their legs. The bus had heaters in the floor too, so the warm air rose and kept the worst of the wind from chilling Mia's cheeks.

Natalie Grant

"Did you wear your Snow Angel socks today?" Lulu asked Ruthie.

"I did," Ruthie said, beaming. "You wouldn't believe what a difference wool socks make when you're standing here in the stairwell and the wind is whipping up past your toes."

"Are you sure you don't have any idea who gave the socks to you?" Mia asked. "Doesn't any passenger stand out? Maybe someone asked you lots of questions, or mentioned your socks a lot?"

"You mean someone other than you girls?" Ruthie waved her comment away. "Nah. I'm just teasing. No one suspicious stands out to me. Like I told the reporters, whoever the Snow Angel is, she is sneaky. I notice just about everything, and I didn't notice a thing about her."

"So you think the Angel is a woman?" Mia asked, noticing that Ruthie had said "she."

"Well, I don't know for sure." Ruthie shrugged. "Seems like a thing a woman would do, but who knows, really."

The bus engine fired up and they began to rumble forward. Sitting on top of the bus reminded Mia of being in London, though this bus felt much different than London's double-deckers.

Ruthie pointed out the sights as they navigated the crowded streets. They passed the Empire State Building, Greenwich Village, and headed toward the

Brooklyn Bridge. Miss Julia snapped photos of the sites and of the girls and their parents. Lulu clowned for the camera, but not as much as she normally would. She kept messing with the things in her backpack. Probably trying to use the kit and be a detective, Mia thought.

"Should we ask Ruthie anything else?" Mia asked Maddie.

"I don't know what to ask," Maddie said. "But I don't think we should give up."

"I agree." Mia tapped her fingers on the blanket, thinking over everything Ruthie had said so far. Ruthie seemed to know every bit of the city's history. The next time Ruthie paused in her tour narration, Mia slipped out of her warm seat and moved closer.

"You know a lot about the history of New York," Mia said.

"True," Ruthie said, turning her bright smile on Mia.

"Has there ever been another campaign like the Snow Angel one? Where someone gave secret gifts across the city?"

"Nothing quite like it," Ruthie said. "There have been public acts of kindness campaigns, like the Give a Hug campaign. Or the one that Mark Malkoff—he's a local comedian and filmmaker—did, but I can't think of a secret gift-giver. And keeping a secret in New York for this long . . . well, it's not easy to do. At least, with so many people watching."

"Do you think the Snow Angel rode this bus?"

Natalie Grant

"Must have," Ruthie said, shaking her head.

"You didn't see a family with two girls who asked a lot of questions, did you?" Mia asked.

Ruthie frowned. "Well, I've talked to a lot of families, and many do have two girls, but . . . no. I wouldn't say there were any that stood out. What makes you so curious about the Snow Angel?" She addressed the question to Maddie and Lulu, who had now moved closer to join the conversation.

"We thought we could solve the mystery of who the Snow Angel really is," Maddie said. "We thought it would be fun to figure it out while we're visiting New York."

"Well, don't forget some of the fun is in the looking," Ruthie said. "It's not only about the solving."

"True," Mia said.

"Mmph." Lulu returned to her seat and reached back into her bag. Clearly, she wanted to get back to her own looking, even if it meant peering over the side of the bus with a magnifying glass. Mia decided not to point out how useless this kind of looking was, for so many reasons.

"Thank you for your help," Mia said to Ruthie.

"Any time," Ruthie said, and then her eyes lit up. "You know what I do have . . ." She pulled a paper snowflake out of her tour binder. "I'd like to give this to you girls, a souvenir of the city."

"But, it's your snowflake," Mia said. "From the Snow Angel . . ."

112

"I'm quite content with my warm socks," Ruthie said. "And I have a feeling you girls might make better use of this snowflake than I will."

Mia cradled the snowflake in her hands. "Thank you!"

"Yes, thank you," Maddie said.

"And . . ." Ruthie said with a flourish of her arm, "we're here at Castle Clinton, where you can board the ferry out to the Statue of Liberty."

"This is our stop," Dad called.

"You can hop on any of our buses and ride uptown when you're done," Ruthie said. "On the way back, make sure to see One World Trade Center."

Mia pressed the snowflake flat in the book she'd brought along. She knew they wouldn't find any real clues on the snowflake—like fingerprints—but still. The Snow Angel had held this snowflake in her hands. And now it was here, in Mia's own hands. It was a connection, even if it was only a small one, and it made her feel hopeful.

"Maybe we'll find the Snow Angel after all," Mia said to Maddie as they descended the steps back toward the street.

Maddie grinned. "Maybe!"

SEVENTEEN

Castle Clinton wasn't anything like a castle—it was more of a fortress. Inside the round walls, the sky opened up over their heads. The girls peeked through the gaps in the fortress wall to see out over New York Harbor. Soon, it was time to board their ferry. National Park rangers ran the castle and the ferry, so the ferry's crew wore official park ranger gear. The uniforms, and especially the wide-brimmed hats, looked a little out of place on the ferry.

As they waited to board, Mia could see the Statue of Liberty far across the harbor. From this distance, it was difficult to make out any details beyond her recognizable shape. Good thing they were riding the ferry out to take a closer look. The ferry had two levels. Heat filled the enclosed lower level, so the Glimmer family and Miss Julia decided to stake out seats where they could see out the windows for now. The top deck looked cold. Most of the other passengers did the same, so by the time the ferry doors closed, the room was stuffed full of people.

The ferry's engine rumbled to life, and they began to back away from the dock.

One of the rangers picked up the microphone. "We're on our way to Liberty Island, where the Statue of

Liberty has been welcoming travelers for more than 125 years. The Statue of Liberty was a gift from the people of France to honor the 100th anniversary of the signing of the Declaration of Independence. In fact, when you take a closer look, you'll see that Lady Liberty holds a tablet in her left hand. What you won't be able to see from below is that her tablet is inscribed July 4, 1776."

A man in one of the front rows raised a hand. "Wasn't the Statue of Liberty designed by Eiffel? The same man who designed the Eiffel Tower?"

The ranger nodded, acknowledging the question. "Yes. Eiffel's ingenious skeletal design allows Lady Liberty to move and sway in the wind. Otherwise, she'd crack from standing out in the elements in the harbor. The way things are now, we believe she can stand for another 1,000 years."

The same man raised his hand again. "And didn't the United States have to pay for the pedestal, even though the Statue of Liberty was a gift from France?"

This man was starting to remind Mia of the kids in class who asked questions to show off that they already knew the answers. She elbowed Maddie and raised her eyebrows toward the man. Maddie nodded in total agreement.

The ranger didn't seem to mind. Probably having someone asking questions he knew the answers to was better than a ferry full of people who didn't pay attention. That must happen sometimes too.

"True," the ranger said. "And raising the funds to build the pedestal proved harder than you'd think. At first, Americans didn't realize what an important symbol Lady Liberty would become for our country. But since the time she was installed, her lantern has welcomed many immigrants to our shores. In fact, between 1886 and 1924, almost 14 million immigrants came through this harbor. They came from England, Ireland, Italy, Germany, and many of the Scandinavian countries, and passed the Statue of Liberty on their way to Ellis Island, which is right next to Liberty Island."

"Can't we go outside?" Lulu asked, wiggling in her seat.

"I'll take you," Miss Julia offered.

The girls all went—out the door and up the steps to the top deck. There weren't many people on the top deck, just a few clusters here and there, looking over the railings. The girls made their way to one railing to look at the city, and then to the other to look at the Statue of Liberty. She was coming closer all the time. Lulu rummaged around in her backpack and pulled out her magnifying glass.

"What do you need to see close up?" Mia asked, puzzled. "We're on the ferry. Everything is out in the distance."

Lulu ignored this and started investigating the railing. Sometimes—many times, actually—Mia didn't understand her little sister. No point in making a big deal about it, though. She turned back to look over the water. Behind her, Lulu started to sing her cha-cha-cha song from this morning. Mia decided to ignore it, focusing instead on the wind in her hair and the salty mist on her cheeks. Just because Lulu wanted their attention didn't mean she had to have it all the time.

"Lulu, be careful near the railing," Miss Julia warned.

"Cha-cha-cha!" Lulu said.

Mia rolled her eyes, and then caught herself. *God, please help me be patient*, she prayed.

"Let's take a picture of you girls with the city behind you," Miss Julia said.

Mia was grateful for the distraction. She and Maddie posed and smiled, and Miss Julia snapped a few photos.

"Let's try a silly one," Miss Julia said.

As they posed and she took the photo, Lulu's song finally stopped. Mia breathed a sigh of relief, looking at the few other people up on the top deck. At least everyone would have a break now from her sister's constant noise.

"Lulu, come take a picture with us," Miss Julia called over her shoulder.

Lulu didn't come right away, and they all turned to look for her. For one frightening moment, Mia couldn't see her sister. Her heart started to thud. What if Lulu had tumbled over the railing into the water? She was about to run and look into the water when Lulu

suddenly appeared. She came out from behind the
white structure at the front of the ferry that looked like
an enclosed little room. Mia assumed the room was for
the ship's captain.

"Don't scare me like that!" Miss Julia crossed the
deck and wrapped an arm around Lulu's shoulders. She
brought Lulu over to join the girls and said, "Smile!"

She adjusted her angle to take a few more pictures.
The wind bit at their cheeks, so they soon decided to go
back inside to sit with Mom and Dad. Everyone watched
out the salt-crusted windows. Even though the view
wasn't nearly as nice as the one on the top deck, it was a
relief to be inside, away from the cold. Out the window,
Liberty Island approached, but they still had about half
the harbor to cross. The boat rocked in the waves.

"Mia, would you like to put together the scavenger
hunt for tomorrow?" Miss Julia pulled out her copy of
From the Mixed-Up Files.

"But you'll spoil the book," Maddie said. "If you talk
about what happens next, I mean. Remember, I haven't
read the whole book yet!"

"We'll be quiet," Miss Julia said. "And we'll choose
items that don't give the story away."

"We promise not to listen." Lulu covered her ears
and started to sing.

A few people turned to look.

"How about you come sit with me?" Mom suggested,
making room for Maddie and Lulu by her window.

Once the other girls were out of earshot, Mia told Miss Julia, "Let's look for that fountain where Claudia and Jamie took baths. What was it called?"

Miss Julia flipped through the book to find that passage. "Looks like it's called the Fountain of the Muses."

Mia thought hard, trying to remember. "And there were some works of art that Claudia liked. A necklace, I think, and . . . a stone statue of a cat?"

Miss Julia flipped through the book, jotting notes.

"That's three, right?" Mia asked.

"The fountain, the jewelry of Princess Sit Hathor Yunet, a bronze cat in the Egyptian Wing. Yes, three," Miss Julia said.

"We need more," Mia said. "They slept in a bed with curtains and hid their stuff in a giant urn."

Miss Julia flipped through to find those pages, and then studied them more closely. "Yes, but it doesn't tell us which bed or which urn."

"Oh," Mia said.

"We can look for a bed with curtains and any large urn. That way, we can't look them up on a map—you'll have to actually hunt," Miss Julia said.

"I want there to be ten things," Mia said. "Is that too many?"

"Not at all. You have five. How about I research and add five more? I'll choose things you girls might like to see in the museum, even if they weren't in the book," Miss Julia suggested.

EIGHTEEN

We're here!" Maddie said, pointing out the window. As if to agree, the ferry bumped up against the dock with a thump. The rangers opened the doors and got to work securing the ferry.

"Welcome to Liberty Island," one of them said. "This way, everyone!"

On Liberty Island, a grand, paved path led to the Statue of Liberty's pedestal. Trees lined the walk, and off to one side, statues were tucked between the trees.

"What are those?" Mia asked.

Miss Julia checked the map. "It's a sculpture garden. We should go look closer after we've explored the pedestal."

"What's there to explore?" Maddie asked.

"There's a museum in the building under the statue," Mom said.

Dad laced his fingers through Mom's. "As an extra treat, we get to visit the top of the pedestal. It isn't as high as the Statue of Liberty's crown, but it's still pretty high. We'll see excellent views of the city from there."

Quiet fell over the group as they approached Lady Liberty. Right now, she faced away from them, but even seeing her from the back and up close was fascinating. For one thing, she was at least three times larger than any statue Mia had ever seen. In all the pictures Mia had seen of the Statue of Liberty, she'd taken all those folds in her gown for granted. Now, she realized how much patience it must have taken to create them. The statue's beauty surprised Mia, and there also was an air about the whole island that made her feel quiet, respectful, thoughtful. And it seemed like it had the same effect on everyone in the group that was there, not just Mia or the rest of the Glimmers. The Statue of Liberty had become more than a work of art. She was a symbol for all those immigrants the ranger had talked about, and also for every American. She was a symbol of freedom. Well, actually, liberty, but Mia was pretty sure those words meant almost the same thing.

Mia soaked up the silence. Then, she frowned. She honestly couldn't remember a time when their family had been together and things had been this quiet. She glanced over at Lulu, who was walking with her head down, not even looking up at the statue.

"Lulu, is everything okay?" Maddie had noticed Lulu's quietness too.

Lulu nodded, but her nod wasn't all that convincing. Mia decided to leave it alone. At least Lulu wasn't throwing a fit about something or dancing around and singing, distracting the other people at the statue. Maybe she wasn't all that interested in the Statue of Liberty. Maybe she was tired. Or maybe she was thinking about the girls' concert on Friday. Guilt panged through Mia at the thought.

Miss Julia wrapped an arm around Lulu and started pointing things out to her. Mia seized her chance to talk to Maddie without Lulu overhearing.

"Maddie." Mia caught Maddie's arm and waited until everyone else was a few steps ahead. "I've been thinking about Friday morning."

"And the concert?" Maddie asked, nodding. "I have too."

"Should we ask if Lulu could sing with us?" Mia asked. "If we perform her song, it would only make sense for her to sing with us."

"But would you be okay with that?" Maddie asked. "We just sing backup in that song, nothing special. And we're already doing her song for the concert on Friday night in Times Square."

Mia swallowed hard. The minute Jennifer had suggested they sing on Friday, Mia had pictured singing one of the songs that featured her. From there, she hadn't been able to stop her mind from leap-frogging from possibility to possibility. What if someone important heard them and asked them to record another album . . . What if they could someday be famous just like Mom? That word was a problem for her, she knew. Mom had talked to them often about guarding their hearts, about remembering that gifts were from God. One reason Mia had been so excited about the album in the first place was because it wasn't about them. Even though they were doing a thing she'd dreamed of doing—recording an album!—the point was raising money for teens in need, not bringing fame and fortune to the Glimmers.

"I'd be okay with it," Mia said. "But do you think we can trust Lulu to take it seriously? I mean, you know what could happen."

"Yeah," Maddie agreed. "You know how Mom said we should pray for Lulu? I've been doing that, and ever since I started praying, I keep having this thought about *Rise and Shine*. I can't help wondering—?"

"If it's an idea from God?" Mia asked. "To help us start building trust back with Lulu?"

Maddie's mouth tilted up in a half smile. "It doesn't feel like an idea I'd have on my own."

"Yeah." Mia nodded her head. "I think it's the right thing to do. We should ask Mom when Lulu isn't around, though. Just in case Mom says no or it doesn't work out or whatever."

"Okay," Maddie agreed.

"Girls, are you coming?" Dad called.

They hurried to catch up. Inside, the building wasn't nearly as dark as Mia had expected it to be. Outside, the building resembled Castle Clinton, more like a bunker than a building. To her surprise, light poured in windows set high in the walls. For a little while, they wandered through the museum. Exhibits told the stories of immigrants and the history of the construction of the Statue of Liberty. Even though there was an elevator to the top of the pedestal, they climbed the 215 steps to the top.

When they looked out the windows at the New York City skyline across the harbor, Dad asked, "Worth the climb?"

"Worth it!" Mia and Maddie said.

"What do you think, Lulu?" Dad asked.

Lulu nodded and smiled a watery smile.

"How about I take Lulu down in the elevator and out to the sculpture garden?" Miss Julia suggested to the family, seeming to notice that Lulu wasn't her usual self. "I have some snacks. I'll bet you're hungry, Lulu."

Lulu didn't put up any resistance as Miss Julia took her outside. Dad was busy taking photos of the New York skyline. Maddie nudged Mia. It was time.

"Mom, do you think we could ask *Rise and Shine* if they'd let Lulu sing with us on Friday?" Mia asked. "We could sing her song."

Mom looked surprised. "Let's find a place to sit so we can talk about this."

Once she found a bench, she turned to the girls. "Tell me what you're thinking here.

"Lulu has been trying hard lately," Maddie said. "I mean, since the hair mess."

"And it's true that the album is our project, so it was fair for us to be interviewed about it without Lulu," Mia said. "But I'm not sure if it's fair for us to also have a chance to sing on television without her. It seems like a lot of special things for us, and only the ice skating for her."

"Singing on *Rise and Shine* would mean a lot to Lulu," Maddie said. "And she's not saying so, but something is obviously upsetting her. Maybe singing with us would cheer her up."

"Part of me wants to keep punishing her for what she did to our hair, and to not include her. I feel like saying, *'It serves her right,'*" Mia said. "But that seems like a not-very-forgiving attitude."

"True," Mom said. "A sweet gesture like this is a generous way for you to work toward mending things with Lulu. You're offering her the chance to rise to the occasion as well. But are you sure? Once I call Jennifer and put this in motion, it won't be easy to take back."

"We know," Mia said.

"It's still the right thing to do," Maddie said.

"Okay," Mom said. "I'll call Jennifer when we get back to the hotel. Sound good?"

They agreed on it, and then went to find Dad, who was still snapping photo after photo.

"Ready?" Mom asked.

Dad took one last shot. "Ready."

They made their way down the steps and out of the building to find Miss Julia and Lulu. After everyone had a snack in the sculpture garden, they lined up to take a photo in front of the Statue of Liberty.

"Smile, Lulu," Miss Julia said.

Mia glanced at her sister and saw again how uncomfortable she looked. Something was obviously wrong. Maybe having a good attitude about Friday was wearing her out. Plus, they hadn't heard anything about the Snow Angel for hours, so Lulu wasn't distracted by mystery-solving either. Well, soon they'd have good news for Lulu. Maybe they could put all this behind them. At least, Mia hoped so.

NINETEEN

They rode the ferry back across the harbor, and then found another red bus to ride uptown and back to Times Square. They passed Little Italy, Chinatown, and One World Trade Center. The tour guide on this red bus didn't have as many stories as Ruthie, but he shared little tidbits about the city too. Plus, he pointed out a few Snow Angel sites as they passed by.

"Do you have any idea who the Snow Angel might be?" Mia asked as they passed the guide on the way down the stairs and off the bus.

"If I had to guess," he said, "I'd say it's the mayor. Wanting to take part in Light Up New York Week, but not wanting anyone to know it's him. Or I guess some other kind of celebrity. But I'd put money on the mayor."

Mia thought this over as they walked back to the hotel from Times Square. Would it be a satisfying end to the mystery if the Snow Angel was the mayor? Maybe. She hoped whoever the Snow Angel was, his or her reason for giving gifts was kind and meaningful. After all the attention, it would definitely be disappointing to find out the Snow Angel was giving gifts for some selfish reason.

When Mom opened the door to their rooms, she said, "It's been a long day of exploring, and I'm sure you girls are tired. I have a couple phone calls to make, and

Dad wants to take a nap. After we've rested a bit, we can figure out dinner."

"Sounds good!" Mia said, trying to stay excited about sharing the *Rise and Shine* concert with Lulu. She curled up on the bed with her book, and Maddie took out her sketchbook and pencils.

After a few minutes, Mia looked up. The room was too quiet. "Where's Lulu?"

"I have no idea."

"Lulu!" they both called.

No answer. They exchanged a look, and then climbed off the bed to check in Mom and Dad's room. If Mom was calling Jennifer Jensen at *Rise and Shine*, Lulu couldn't be in there, could she?

Mom was finishing up her conversation. She held up a finger, and the girls waited, but Mia didn't feel all that patient. Where was Lulu, anyway?

"Perfect. Thank you, Jennifer," Mom said. "See you tomorrow."

When she hung up the phone, she asked, "What's up?"

"Have you seen Lulu?" Maddie asked.

Mom exchanged a look with Dad and they went into the girls' room, with Mia and Maddie following. Their room wasn't all that big, and it didn't take long for them to notice that the bathroom door was ajar. Now that she was just outside the door, Mia heard Lulu sniffle and then sniffle again.

"Lulu?" Mom nudged the door open.

The shower curtain was pulled around the tub. Gently, Mom pulled it back, and there was Lulu sitting in the empty tub, her arms around her knees.

"I didn't mean to drop it," Lulu said, tears streaming down her face. "I promise, I didn't mean to."

Mia had no idea what Lulu was talking about. "Drop what?"

Lulu burst into loud sobs, and Dad lifted her from the tub. He carried her out of the bathroom, across the girls' room, and took her into their room. No one could understand a thing Lulu was saying through her wails.

"Stay here, girls," Mom said. "Once we've figured out what's happened, we'll be back."

Mom closed the door behind her. Mia stood listening to Lulu's sobs and tried to decipher the garbled things she was saying.

"She dropped what?" Mia asked finally, eyeing the closed door.

Maddie sat on the edge of the bed and swung her legs, staring at her toes.

"What?" Mia demanded, and then opened her book. "She didn't drop the snowflake, because that's right here. She had her whole backpack on the trip, so she could have lost one of her toys, or . . ."

Dad came through the door and closed it behind him with a soft click. Mom stayed with Lulu, who continued to sob and gasp loudly enough that they could hear it through the walls.

"What did she drop?" Mia asked again, feeling exasperated now. She could not keep it out of her voice.

"Mia, come and sit with us." Dad sat on the bed next to Maddie and motioned to the open space.

Mia sat. She tried to quiet the bubbling, boiling anxiety that filled her body, making it nearly impossible to sit still.

"This morning, Lulu came back into the rooms to get her backpack and detective kit right before we left. When she grabbed her bag, she also decided to take the snow globe with her on our trip," Dad said. "So she could look at it without someone telling her to put it away."

For a moment, Mia was speechless. She leaned forward, not believing what Dad was telling them.

"Apparently, while you were taking photos with Miss Julia on the ferry, Lulu was playing around with the snow globe," Dad said. "She started out using her magnifying glass to look at the details, but then she decided to shake the globe and to see how the scene looked with the snow falling."

"Her cha-cha-cha song," Maddie said, and as soon as she said it, Mia remembered it too. Lulu had been singing. Mia had tried to block out the noise. Then, when Lulu had gone all funny and quiet, Mia had noticed, but she hadn't thought that something bad had happened. Something like dropping the snow globe.

"But we didn't hear any glass break," Mia said.

"It was windy," Maddie said, looking at her sister. "We might not have heard it."

"It dropped over the railing, into the water." Dad looked each of the girls in the eyes. "I'm so sorry, girls."

For a moment, no one said anything at all. Mia had no idea what to say. A new wail rose on the other side of the wall, and Dad cast a worried glance at the door. "I need to go check on Mom. When we can, we'll both come back to talk with you."

When he opened the door, Mia heard Lulu gasp out, "It's so hard to be youngest."

"I hear you," Mom said. "When you're the youngest, you're working so hard to be big. I felt that way myself. I was the youngest, you know."

"Will I always be bad?" Lulu asked.

After this, Dad closed the door, and Mia didn't hear Mom's answer. Her anger grew and grew, feeling like it might explode out of her. She picked up a pillow and threw it against the others. "I thought that by praying for us and praying for her, things would get better. And we even included her in the concert . . . and look what she did!" Mia tossed herself face-first onto the bed and buried her face in the pillows.

Maddie's voice was very small as she said, "I don't know how we'll forgive her for this."

"Mmmph," Mia said into the pillows.

They waited, listening to Lulu's sobbing slow, and then quiet. Then they heard Miss Julia's voice, and after a minute or two, the hallway door closing. Mom and Dad came into the girls' room soon after. They sat together on the window seat. Mia pulled herself up beside Maddie and hugged a pillow to her chest.

"We sent Lulu down to the lobby on an errand with Miss Julia so we could talk on our own," Mom said.

Mia didn't know what to say, and apparently Maddie didn't either. The silence stretched until Mia started to feel uncomfortable. What was she supposed to say?

"How are you girls feeling?" Dad asked, finally breaking the silence.

Mia searched around for the right word. Finally, she settled on, "Frustrated."

"Angry," Maddie said, truthfully.

TWENTY

Mia looked at her sister with surprise. It took a lot to make Maddie angry, and maybe more to make her admit she was mad. Mia hadn't been able to say so, but now that Maddie had broken the tension, Mia felt her own anger bubble over the surface too.

"It's like we're supposed to be okay with anything Lulu does because she's the youngest," Maddie said. "But it's not like she doesn't know better."

"She sobs and wails and acts like she's the one who we should all comfort, when we're the ones who don't have the snow globe anymore," Mia said.

"Lulu was wrong to take the snow globe without asking," Mom said. "And you're right. While losing the snow globe felt terrible to Lulu, and it is something she would take back in a heartbeat, her actions hurt both of you."

Maddie pressed her palms against the mattress, as though she could push her anger into the bed and rid herself of it. "It keeps getting worse and worse. We forgive her and try to be nice, like when we bought her the detective kit and included her in *Rise and Shine*. And still, everything she does is worse than the thing she did before."

"I told her not to play with the snow globe," Mia said. "I knew something bad was going to happen."

The words sat there between them, and slowly, Mom started to nod.

"Girls," she said. "I owe you an apology. We talked in the cab about broken trust, about how difficult it is to repair. Unfortunately, now I've broken your trust too. You gave me the snow globe for safekeeping. I didn't tell Lulu it was completely off limits. I put it in my drawer because I thought locking it up in the safe would give Lulu the wrong impression. I heard your concerns about what might happen, but I wanted so much for Lulu to earn back your trust, to make the right decisions, that I did some things that I would change now if I could do them over again."

"It's not your fault!" Maddie hurried to say. "Lulu was the one who took the snow globe and dropped it. I think she's old enough to know what is right and what is wrong."

"No, it's not my fault," Mom agreed. "But I apologize for my part in what happened."

The words *We forgive you* popped into Mia's head, but she realized she couldn't say them. Not yet. She needed to talk to Mom and Dad about the bigger thing, the thing that went far beyond the snow globe.

"You . . ." she started, and then faltered. How did you explain something like this to your mom or dad?

"What is it, Mia?" Dad prodded. "It's okay. You can tell us what you're thinking and feeling. We want you to tell us."

Mia nodded, trying to reframe what she needed to say from an accusation into words that felt more truthful. "I feel like there's this giant space in the family for Lulu and Lulu's feelings. And then there's the tiny space that's left over. And that's the space we get—Maddie and me. And I feel like you expect us to be okay with that, to always make room for Lulu, no matter what."

"It hurts my feelings," Maddie added in a small voice, "when it feels like I matter less than Lulu."

"But we don't . . . We would never . . ." Mom started.

Dad put his arm around Mom. "I so sorry for causing you to feel that way, girls."

Mom nodded, her eyes filling with tears. "You both matter to us so very much."

She went to them then and wrapped her arms around them. Tears started to roll down Mia's face.

"I'm sorry too, girls," Mom said. "So very sorry. What can we do to make this right?"

Mia shook her head and then said, honestly, "I don't know. Lulu isn't going to stop being Lulu."

At this, Maddie choked out a laugh, and Mom and Dad laughed a little too. It felt good to laugh, to let some of the tension dissolve. Mia felt better having admitted her feelings, finally. Now that she'd put them into words, they didn't feel so powerful, so overwhelming. Mom let them go and looked Mia and Maddie each in the eyes.

"I love you girls so much."

"Love you too, Mom," Mia said, and then, not wanting to leave Dad out, she hugged Dad as well. "You're not so bad either."

"No?" He quirked an eyebrow and then pulled her in tight for a hug. He swept Maddie up next, and it felt like a festival of hugs for a moment, until they all settled back down to finish talking. Mia knew they couldn't leave it at that, as much as she'd like to. Mom had asked what she and Dad could do, and Mia wanted to answer. What *could* her parents do?

"When something goes wrong with Lulu," Mia said, slowly, feeling her way, "you tell us how she probably feels. It's not that I don't want to know, but when you tell us how she feels, I feel like I'm supposed to not feel my own feelings anymore. It seems like only her feelings matter."

Maddie nodded, picking up where Mia had left off. "Maybe if you let us be upset for a little while—not that I like being upset, but maybe we need a little space. Like we could take a walk or something."

"I like that idea," Mom said. "Perhaps we could have a family plan, and Lulu would know—we all would know—that each of us need time before we work things out. And even when someone feels upset, they might have to wait until the other person is ready to talk."

Mia thought this plan over. Maybe it would help to have a little more time to think things over before having to fix them.

"You know what I'm proud of you for?" Dad asked. "Today, you were upset with Mom and me, but instead of telling us it was okay, you shared your real feelings with us. That's not easy to do with anyone, and in particular with your parents. But when we know how you truly feel, we can deal with the problem rather than avoid it. I wonder . . . What if you did the same with Lulu? What if you didn't tell her everything is okay all the time? For example, what if you told her how sad, how upset you are about losing the snow globe?"

"She'll cry," Maddie said.

"She will," Dad agreed. "But I think she'd feel worse if you said it was okay, especially since she knows it isn't."

"Plus, you'd be doing what big sisters should do, model a way to be. You're showing Lulu that it's okay to talk about feeling upset. Maybe after a while, she will try it herself." Mom ran her fingers softly against Maddie's cheek. "You never know. Maybe she'll start talking to you about her feelings rather than acting out."

"Or crying," Maddie said.

"Or crying," Mom agreed.

"What did you say to her, Mom?" Mia asked, remembering what she'd overheard from the other bedroom. "When she asked if she'd always be bad?"

"I reminded her that God made her in his image, and that means that she is not bad. The thing is, as long as we're on earth, we have the opportunity to make selfish choices."

"Huh," Mia said, thinking about this. "I guess we all make selfish choices. Big ones, little ones, in-between ones . . ."

"Exactly," Mom agreed.

"You know how you always say the consequences should fit the situation?" Maddie asked. "What will happen to Lulu? I mean, she didn't break a rule, exactly, but she knew she shouldn't take the snow globe out of the drawer."

"It's a difficult one," Mom agreed. "And honestly, I haven't decided yet on Lulu's consequences. No matter what consequences we give her, the worst one is having lost the snow globe. Even once you girls are able to forgive her, I think she will have a difficult time forgiving herself."

Mia shifted uncomfortably on the bed. What she wanted to do and what was most likely the right thing to do were the exact opposite.

"What are you thinking, Mia?" Mom asked.

"I think if we uninvited her to sing with us, even though she doesn't know about it yet, that would be like trying to get even," Mia said.

"I think so too," Maddie said.

Dad nodded. "I do think that changing the plan for the Friday morning concert would be more harmful than helpful to all of you girls. We'll work on some consequences that will include firm boundaries about anything that is off limits for Lulu. I'd like to also give

Lulu the chance to decide on what she'd like to do to restore things between herself and you girls. Sometimes saying sorry just doesn't feel like enough to fix what is broken. I know Lulu wants to fix things, and right now, she's not sure she ever can."

"But right now," Mom said, "what if we take some time, just you girls and us? How about we have a special dinner? Miss Julia and Lulu can order room service, or have dinner somewhere nearby. That way, you can have a little space away from Lulu before talking to her about what happened. What do you say?"

A wave of relief swept through Mia. Somewhere in the back of her mind, she'd been waiting for the door to open at any moment. She'd had no idea how she would pull together the words she'd need to talk to Lulu.

"Yes, please!" she said.

"Perfect!" Maddie agreed.

"Well, what are we waiting for, then?" Dad asked.

Mom called Miss Julia, and then they bundled up and were off. Out on the sidewalk, Mia took Maddie's gloved hand and swung it as they walked.

"I think everything is going to be all right," Mia said, full of a strange happy-sad feeling.

Maddie squeezed her hand in agreement. "Me too."

TWENTY-ONE

L ulu was already in bed when they came back to the hotel. She and Miss Julia were watching television in the girls' room. On the screen, a reporter was standing in front of a map of New York City that was marked with snowflakes.

"More Snow Angel news!" Maddie said, hurrying in to hear the report.

All week, the frequency of gift-giving had been multiplying. It seemed the Snow Angel was everywhere at once, giving gift after gift—today, eight—from one corner of the city to the other.

The reporter moved on from the Snow Angel report to talk about Light Up New York Week in general. Teams of volunteers had visited shelters and other sites across the city, doing all kinds of helpful work. Some had repainted, others had done deep cleaning. A few construction companies had sent team members to remodel bathrooms and offices. Waiting rooms in public health clinics, police stations, and service organizations had been freshened up. It seemed that everyone had done some closet cleaning and come up with shoes and blankets and coats they no longer needed. At this point, the shelters that distributed these necessities were overflowing with stock.

"Just two nights from now," the reporter added, "is Solidarity Sleep-Out. High-powered executives, young professionals, and many others are sleeping outside to raise awareness for the youth of our city who do not have anywhere to sleep. This event, sponsored by Covenant House, kicks off with a concert in Times Square. The concert will be lit by thousands of candles. In fact, this event was the inspiration for our Light Up New York Week. As we've seen, compassion and care for others has spilled into every corner of our city."

Miss Julia clicked the television off and stood to go. "Friday night will be a special night. I can't wait to cheer you girls on."

"Climb into bed," Mom said. "We'll come kiss you good night in a few minutes."

Mia nodded at Mom. They'd agreed on the way home that she and Dad would give Mia and Maddie a few minutes to talk with Lulu. They didn't want to go to bed with unspoken frustration between them.

Mom closed the door, and Mia and Maddie climbed onto the bed. Lulu closed her eyes, pretending she was asleep. She cracked one eye open to see if they were looking. When she saw they were, she sighed and sat up.

"I'm sorry," she said, picking at a thread in her comforter.

"Lulu." Mia breathed in and blew out a big breath. "I'm really sad about the snow globe. It was special—a one-of-a-kind."

Lulu nodded, acknowledging this, tears starting to run down her cheeks.

"I'm sad too." Maddie pulled a pillow into her lap. "I wish I could tell you that it's okay, and that we're not upset, but that wouldn't be the truth."

"Actually, we haven't always told you the truth," Mia said. "Sometimes I've told you 'it's okay' when it's really not. I'm sorry, Lulu. It's important for me to tell you the truth."

"I'm sorry too," Maddie said. "I don't like to fight, and sometimes I say it's okay so that everything will go back to the way I want it to be."

"I want everything to be okay," Lulu said.

"We do too," Mia said.

No one said anything for a moment. Mia traced circles on the pillow beside her.

"I forgive you, Lulu," Mia said. "But I don't think everything will go back to the way it was before."

Lulu tilted her head, obviously surprised and a little confused by this. "What do you mean?"

"Well, you can't un-drop the snow globe," Mia said. "And we can't forget that you took it out of the drawer, where it was supposed to be safe. Probably the next time we have something special that we want to keep safe, we won't leave it out like that."

"Because you don't trust me?" Lulu asked, blinking hard.

"Unfortunately, trust isn't like forgiveness," Maddie said. "You can forgive someone just by choosing, but trust takes time to build up."

"You've always just said 'I forgive you' before," Lulu said.

"This isn't different," Maddie said. "We *do* forgive you."

"But we also need to tell you the truth. And the truth is that even though we forgive you, we can't completely trust you yet," Mia said.

After that, no one said anything for a minute. Mia wondered if her words had been too harsh. Still, she'd needed to say them. The sharp anger in her chest had been loosening ever since she'd started telling Lulu the truth.

"Lulu, we want you to be honest with us too. Like about *Rise and Shine*. We know it's a big deal to you that we're singing on Friday. You're pretending that's okay with you, but we know it's not."

"But I don't deserve to sing on *Rise and Shine*," Lulu said, her lower lip starting to tremble.

"Not really," Mia said. "But I'm not sure we deserve to, either. It's just a special opportunity that came up."

"The point is," Maddie said, "we want you to tell us when you're upset. Or try to, at least. And we will try to tell you too."

Lulu nodded. "When I heard Jennifer ask you to sing on the show, I cried a little."

Mia looked over at Maddie, checking to see if this was the right time. Maddie nodded.

"So, Lulu," Mia said, "today, Mom called Jennifer Jensen at *Rise and Shine* and asked if we could sing your song on the show. With you singing lead."

Lulu looked up, her eyes full of hope and disbelief.

Maddie smiled. "And she said yes."

"And I still get to?" Lulu asked. "Even after . . . ?"

"If there's one thing I trust you with," Mia said, "it's that song. You are amazing in that song, Lulu."

"But no going wild on camera," Maddie warned. "Promise?"

"I promise," Lulu said, and then crossed her heart. "No, truly, I promise. I'll be on my best, best, best behavior."

Mia quirked an eyebrow. "Best?"

"Yes!" Lulu launched herself at the bed to give both of her sisters hugs.

Mom cracked open the door. "What's this I hear? I thought you were going to bed?"

Lulu scrambled back onto the rollaway and pulled her covers up to her chin. "Yep, right now!"

They all lay back, and Mom kissed Lulu, then Maddie and Mia.

"I'm proud of you," Mom whispered in Mia's ear.

Mia closed her eyes. The feeling of Mom's pride, Dad's love, Lulu's happiness, Maddie's honesty, and her own twinge of sadness and anger over having lost the snow globe all mixed together. If she could do it over, she'd definitely choose not to lose the snow globe. But even though what she gained couldn't be held in her hands like a snow globe, it still seemed significant.

Thank you, she prayed silently. *Thank you for giving me the words. And, God? Please make me patient tomorrow. Oh, and bless Lulu too.*

TWENTY-TWO

Mom came in and woke them up the next morning, kissing each girl on the forehead. "Today's a big day. First, we're going to the Met. Then, later this afternoon, we have a rehearsal booked at *Rise and Shine*, so you're ready for the concert tomorrow."

"Can we go now?" Lulu asked, leaping out of bed, her hair sticking up in clumps.

Everyone laughed. It felt good to start the day with a laugh, especially after all of yesterday's tension.

"We can go as soon as you're dressed," Mom said. "Well, and as soon as you brush your hair. And teeth."

"And wash our faces!" Maddie reminded her.

"Right," Mom said.

They clambered over one another to get out of bed, and piled into the bathroom. Everywhere they went, it seemed like everyone else was exactly in that spot too. Soon enough, they were all dressed and ready to go.

"Coffee!" Dad said, causing all the girls to groan.

"How about we take a cab over to the Met, and have breakfast somewhere close to the museum?" Mom suggested. "And coffee," she added, before Dad could grumble.

"Can I bring my detective kit?" Lulu asked.

"I don't think we're going to find the Snow Angel," Mia said. As she said it, she felt the reality of her words settling in. Today, they'd be at the Met for a few hours, and then at the *Rise and Shine* studio. Tomorrow, they had the televised concert in the morning and the Light Up New York performance in the evening. How would they have any more time to sleuth? The window of opportunity seemed to have passed.

"You could use it for the scavenger hunt, though," Maddie suggested.

The thought of the scavenger hunt filled Mia with a little fizz of happiness. Maybe they couldn't solve a real mystery in New York, but the scavenger hunt was a kind of mystery. Sort of.

Lulu packed her detective kit into her backpack, and they knocked on Miss Julia's door. "Are you ready for a scavenger hunt?" she asked the girls, waving her list as she opened her door.

"Yes!" they said, and Lulu did a little on-the-spot dance.

"Off we go," Mom said.

The cab ride didn't take all that long, hardly long enough for Dad to decide which coffee shop he wanted to try. But in the end, he chose one. The girls thought he'd made an excellent choice, because the baked goods case had Belgian waffles.

"Just like Captain Swashbuckler's Adventure Park!" Lulu cheered.

Mom also found fruit and yogurt to round out their breakfast. They sat at a table near the window, watching snow drift slowly onto the sidewalk. Each flake melted the minute it touched down. Mia had just taken a bite of her sweet, crunchy waffle when Maddie leaned forward, staring out the window, curiosity written all over her face.

"What?" Mia asked.

"Do you see that woman? With the sunglasses and hat, and the way-too-full bags? Come over here, Mia, and look."

"Girls, don't stare," Mom warned, glancing over her shoulder.

Mia hurried around the table to look, and Lulu crowded in too.

"She keeps looking over her shoulder," Maddie said. "Like she doesn't want anyone to notice her."

"Like she has a secret!" Lulu said, bouncing on her toes.

"What do you think she has in her bags?" Maddie asked.

"You don't really think she could be the Snow Angel, do you?" Mia asked. "I mean, she could just be finishing up a shopping trip and she bought too much, right?"

"But look. There, she did it again. Do you see how she keeps looking back? You can tell she's not happy waiting at that crosswalk."

"What are we waiting for?" Lulu asked, springing away and toward the door.

"Oh no, no, no," Miss Julia said, catching her. "Where are you off to?"

"To follow the Snow Angel!" Lulu said.

"Please, Mom, can we go? Just for a second? Just to see?" Mia asked.

Mom seemed at a loss for words. She looked questioningly at Dad.

"You know what?" Dad pushed back his chair. "I'll take you. Let's go and see what's going on."

"Yes, yes, yes!" Lulu said, pumping her fist in the air.

Mia and her sisters followed Dad out the door and down the block. The crosswalk light had just changed, and the woman was hurrying across. The light started to flash orange, counting down. Mia wanted to jaywalk. They might not make it all the way to the crosswalk, and if they didn't get there in time, the woman would get away. If she did, how would they ever know whether she was the Snow Angel?

As they reached the walk, Dad put his arm out to keep them from crossing. Seconds before, the light had changed to red. Even though Mia knew it wasn't safe, she couldn't help feeling frustrated.

"Can't we just walk? The cars don't hit pedestrians here," she said.

Dad shook his head. "I'm definitely not risking the lives of all three of my beautiful daughters on that chance."

Anticipation dissolved out of Mia, making her feel suddenly hollow. She'd been ready to accept they wouldn't find the Snow Angel. Now, they'd come so close. What if they were watching the Snow Angel walk away right now? How long would they have to wait for the next light?

"Look, Mia!" Lulu pulled on Mia's arm and pointed.

The woman had stopped about halfway down the block and was waiting at the bus stop. She'd set her bags down on a bench.

"She's taking something out of her bag!" Maddie said.

Everyone leaned forward, wondering what it would be—a blanket, a coat, maybe socks, or even something else. No one expected it to be a purse, stuffed with tissue paper. As they watched, the woman pulled out the tissue and put it in the nearby trash can. Then, she took a few other items out of the bag—a makeup bag, a couple fancy boxes that probably held lipstick or mascara or eyeshadow, and a fancy leather-looking notebook and pen.

"She's packing up her purse?" Lulu asked, disappointed.

"That seems to be what's happening," Dad said.

The light changed, but no one moved.

"Should we go see?" Dad asked.

"No," Mia said, and the others shook their heads.

"She's obviously not the Snow Angel," Maddie said. "I just figured her bags were full of gifts."

"They were," Mia said. "It's just that they were gifts for herself."

"Yeah." Maddie sounded as disappointed as Mia felt.

"On the bright side, I'll bet my coffee isn't cold yet," Dad said.

"And we have waffles!" Lulu said, already in motion back toward the coffee shop.

"Hold up," Dad said, catching up with her.

Mia and Maddie hurried to join them. Soon, they were back to their breakfast. They explained what they'd seen to Mom and Miss Julia.

"Too bad," Miss Julia said. "But remember, we do still have the scavenger hunt. That's like a mystery."

"Kind of," Mia said. She had to admit it was pretty fun thinking about seeing everything at the Met that Claudia and Jamie had seen. Plus, she couldn't wait to see what surprises Miss Julia had included in the hunt just for her.

"Ready?" Lulu asked, her mouth still full of her last bite.

"A few more minutes," Dad said, showing her his half-full mug.

Lulu wiggled and squirmed, waiting for Dad and everyone else to finish. Mia felt impatient herself, and excited to get to the museum.

"All right," Dad said, looking around the table and making sure everyone was finished. "Now we can go to the Met."

"Yay, yay, yay!" Lulu said, leaping to her feet. "The Glimmer girls are on the case!"

TWENTY-THREE

People clustered in clumps in the Met's Great Hall, removing damp gloves, hats, and scarves and inspecting museum maps.

"We're doing a scavenger hunt in that?" Lulu's eyes widened as she took in the many colors and numbers that filled the complicated map.

"How big is the Met, anyway?" Maddie asked.

"Two million square feet," Miss Julia said, checking her phone. "And the collection here has more than two million works of art."

Mia blinked at her. Two million? She had no idea what two million square feet even meant. Big. Enormous. Too large to imagine.

"So, bigger than the London Art Gallery?" Maddie asked.

"Yes." Miss Julia tapped her phone screen, checking facts. "Wow. Maddie, the London Art Gallery is 12,260 square feet. So that means"—she checked the numbers on her phone's calculator—"that this building would hold more than thirteen London Art Galleries."

"And we have to walk through all of it?" Lulu's face wrinkled in concern.

Mom laughed. "Don't worry, we won't try to see the whole thing today. We'll count this as a reason to come back to New York."

"So, what are we looking for in that scavenger hunt of yours?" Dad asked.

Miss Julia passed the list to Mia, who read the list aloud.

1. The Fountain of the Muses
2. The jewelry of Princess Sit Hathor Yunet
3. A bronze cat in the Egyptian Wing
4. An ornate bed with curtains
5. A giant urn
6. King Henry VIII's armor
7. *The Little Fourteen-Year-Old Dancer* by Edgar Degas
8. *Woman with a Lute* by Johannes Vermeer
9. *The Manneport* by Claude Monet
10. *Washington Crossing the Delaware* by Emanuel Leutze

"What's a man-e-port?" Lulu asked, sounding the word out.

"I think Maddie will especially like that one," Miss Julia said. "I put that one on the list for her."

"Okay, number one," Lulu said, ready to take off. "Where's the Fountain of the Muses?"

"I'm not sure we should go in list order," Mia said. "We don't want to have to wander all over the museum."

"Good thinking," Dad said.

The Great Hall didn't offer any places to sit down, so they climbed the giant stone staircase to look for a bench. They found one positioned in front of a few paintings and sat to make a plan. Miss Julia let the girls use her phone to map out where each piece of art generally should be. Each room was numbered. The colors on the museum map showed the categories of each wing, such as the Greek and Roman Art wing or European Paintings. Soon, they'd found everything on the list, except the Fountain of the Muses.

"It looks like it's not installed here anymore." Mia sighed. Seeing the fountain had been the thing she'd looked forward to most.

"So the hunt is ruined?" Lulu blew out a sigh of exasperation. "We didn't find the Snow Angel, and now we can't even win the scavenger hunt?"

"I'll bet there's a fountain somewhere in this museum with pennies in it," Dad said. "What if we swap that item for any fountain?"

The girls looked at one another, uncertain. On the one hand, Mia felt the whole point of a scavenger hunt was finding the things on the list. Still, they'd made the list up themselves, and there was no reason they couldn't change one.

"As long as we don't change any others along the way," Mia said. "Or we don't win."

"What do we win, if we find them all?" Lulu wanted to know.

"A hug and a kiss?" Dad suggested, eyes twinkling.

"Maybe one souvenir each from the gift shop?" Maddie asked.

"I think that's fair," Mom said.

They shook on it, and then they were off toward the Egyptian Wing. Like the London Art Gallery, the Met was a maze of galleries. They couldn't walk directly to the Egyptian Wing without passing through other galleries. They wound through room after room of paintings. Maddie stopped every once in a while to look at one of the paintings, but Mia wasn't very interested. None of the paintings on the list were in this gallery. This gallery was full of European paintings from a different era than the ones on their list. Most of these were older, and many of them were yellowed with age.

Finally, they stepped out of the maze into a large, open gallery. Two hallways stretched the length of the room, overlooking the downstairs cafe and an indoor courtyard filled with statues. Here was an interesting room. Mia slowed down to take it all in. The floor-to-ceiling windows looked out over Central Park, where snow was starting to stick to the ground.

"Come on, come on!" Lulu grabbed Mia's arm and held the map two inches from her nose. "The Egyptian Wing is this way."

"I don't think we meant to skip over everything that wasn't on the list," Mia grumbled.

"We haven't found *anything* on the list yet," Lulu said, complaint lacing her voice. "Come on."

She didn't have to worry for long. Across the gallery, they found themselves in the American Wing. It wasn't hard to find *Washington Crossing the Delaware*. The painting took up an entire enormous wall. Mia had never seen a painting so big, and she couldn't imagine what it would be like to try to paint something like it.

"Do you think the artist stood on a ladder? And how did they frame it?" Maddie wondered.

"The painting is about twelve by twenty-one feet," Miss Julia said. "That's bigger than your average bedroom."

They took the steps down, and soon found themselves in another giant gallery with floor-to-ceiling windows.

"What is that?" Lulu asked.

The room held a stone temple. Miss Julia read the description aloud. "The Temple of Dendur, an Egyptian temple built around 15 B.C."

"Look at all those hieroglyphics," Maddie said.

"A fountain!" Lulu said, taking off across the room before Miss Julia could catch her.

Sure enough, they'd found a fountain, complete with coins. They marked it off the list and headed into the Egyptian Wing. The princess's jewelry and the giant urn weren't difficult to find either.

"So that's what an urn is," Lulu said when they found it.

They had to look harder for the stone cat, but soon they'd found that too. Next, they found their way into the Gallery of Arms and Armor and spotted King Henry VIII's armor. They decided to walk through a few rooms that may have a bed in them on their way across the museum. As they wound through room after room toward the 19th and Early 20th Century European Paintings and Sculptures, they found one. Jackpot!

"That's seven!" Lulu said, crossing the bed off the list.

The 19th and 20th Century gallery was just beyond. Soon, they'd crossed the Vermeer off the list and had found the beautiful statue of the dancer by Degas.

"This one is my favorite." Lulu mirrored the position of the statue and posed for a picture.

"We're almost done!" Mia said. "All we have left is the *Manneport* by Monet. What does Manneport mean, anyway?"

Miss Julia shook her head. "I'm not telling. It's a surprise for Maddie."

So, Maddie led the way as they searched. When they found the seascape painting, Mia understood why Miss Julia had added it to the list for Maddie. The painting depicted a natural arch cut into a cliff, done in Monet's typical splattered style.

"It's like *Sun-Splattered Afternoon*!" Maddie said, breaking into a giant smile.

It did look remarkably like the painting they'd all loved, but which had been particularly special to Maddie, in the London Art Gallery.

"And that's ten!" Lulu said, crossing the last item off the list with a flourish.

"Congratulations!" Dad said.

"Thank you for the scavenger hunt," Mia said, hugging Miss Julia. It felt nice to have solved a puzzle, even though the bigger puzzle, the mystery of the Snow Angel, remained beyond them.

"What do you say we go have a little lunch and then make our choices in the gift shop?" Mom suggested.

Mia's feet were sore from all that walking. She knew Maddie and Lulu must feel the same way. Everyone agreed, and they made their way back toward the cafe.

TWENTY-FOUR

After a lunch of sandwiches and soup, they went to the gift shop. No one had any trouble choosing a souvenir. Maddie chose a tiny watercolor kit in a wooden box. Lulu chose a miniature figurine of the Degas dancer. Mia found a snow globe with Central Park's *Alice in Wonderland* statue inside. It wasn't the special snow globe from *Rise and Shine*, but still, it was a snow globe. Mia loved the way the sparkling snow settled on and around the statue.

Outside, the snow had started to come down a little harder. Still, Lulu begged to have a chance to see Central Park, and especially Mia's *Alice in Wonderland* statue. The park was beautiful, with a dusting of white covering the grassy hills and paths. Little hats of snow rested on the statues that Mia could see out the window.

"How far is the *Alice in Wonderland* statue?" Dad asked.

Miss Julia looked it up on her phone. "It looks like it should only take about eight minutes to walk there through the park from here. But, listen to this! In total, Central Park has fifty-eight miles of paths."

"Sounds like we lucked out to be close to *Alice in Wonderland*, then," Mom said. "I think there's time to go see the statue. We have about an hour before we need to find a cab to go over to the *Rise and Shine* studio for your rehearsal."

"I'm going to be on television, I'm going to be on television," Lulu chanted, dancing out the door and into the snowy park.

Mom and Dad exchanged a look, but then Mom took Dad's hand, letting Lulu dance and sing. Mia agreed they might as well let Lulu be excited. Maybe it was good for her to get some of this excitement out of her system now before they were actually in the studio. And, honestly, Mia could have danced and sung right along with her little sister. Singing on television was a big deal, and even if they weren't doing one of Mia's special songs, she couldn't wait for the experience.

Along the path, they scooped up snow and tossed snowballs at one another. Dad kept hiding behind trees and ambushing them with snowball attacks. Finally, the three girls decided to team up against him. Once it was three against one, Dad gave in and called a truce. They agreed, but not until they'd pelted him with snowballs one more time.

"There it is!" Lulu pointed out the bronze statue with the familiar *Alice in Wonderland* characters.

"Go ahead, we'll be right behind you," Mom said.

The girls rushed over to the statue, and then circled it, taking in the details.

"The Mad Hatter," Maddie said.

"And the March Hare," Mia added.

"And the Dormouse!" Lulu motioned to the little mouse, who sat on a small mushroom next to the one Alice sat on.

"Do you think that's the Cheshire Cat?" Maddie asked, pointing out the cat in the tree.

"Then who is that?" Lulu asked, nodding at the cat on Alice's lap.

"Didn't Alice have a cat back home?" Mia asked.

"Exactly," Miss Julia said, coming up from behind them. "That's Dinah, Alice's cat. And you know, girls, the artist actually meant for this statue to be touched and climbed on. Would you like to climb up and have your picture taken?"

Climbing up was easier said than done in the snow, but with a little help from Dad, they all managed to clamber up and pose for pictures. Mia's favorite was the silly picture where they all pretended to sip imaginary tea with their pinkies—and noses—up in the air. The girls wanted to play on the statue a little longer, but Mom and Dad wanted to see the lake, which was close by.

"Go ahead," Miss Julia said. "I'll stay with the girls."

Mia, Maddie, and Lulu stayed on the statue a little longer. When their fingers started to feel frozen through their gloves, they climbed down.

Miss Julia rubbed their hands to help warm up their fingers, and then asked, "Anybody want a snack?"

She brushed snow off a bench and held out a variety of packages of dried fruit snacks so the girls could

choose their favorite flavor. Mia chose strawberry and so did Lulu, but Maddie chose raspberry.

Across the grass, a woman laying on a bench caught Mia's eye. She seemed to be fast asleep, though Mia couldn't imagine how she could be in this cold.

"If I were the Snow Angel," she said to Maddie, "I'd want to help that woman."

"What would you give her?" Maddie asked. "Just a blanket?"

"Or a new coat. Or maybe a giant umbrella to prop up and keep the snow off," Mia said, looking away, not wanting to stare at the woman. Even though the woman was asleep—maybe because she was asleep—it didn't seem right to keep watching her.

"Hey!" Lulu said, her voice sharp and cutting across the park's quiet.

Mia turned to her little sister. "Lulu, what—"

But Lulu didn't pay Mia any attention. Instead, she stared toward the woman.

"Lulu, don't stare," Mia said.

"That girl," Lulu said, squinting across the park. "She just left a blanket. And a bag. And I think . . . yes. She just left a snowflake."

"A snowflake?" Mia asked, whipping her head back to look.

"A snowflake," Lulu repeated.

"But that means . . ." Maddie said.

Natalie Grant

"Who is that woman she's heading toward?" Mia asked. "Her mom?"

"She can't be the Snow Angel," Maddie said, her brow furrowed. "She's just a kid."

Lulu completely ignored this. "Hey!" she shouted, as she took off running. "You're the Snow Angel!"

The girl looked up at her mom in alarm, and after her mom nodded, she jogged toward Maddie, Mia, and Lulu.

"Shhh," she said, as she came closer.

"But you're the Sn—"

"Shhhh!" she said, more insistently, glancing over her shoulder.

Mia looked between the girl and Lulu, not sure whether to urge Lulu to stay quiet or to join her in shouting. Of all the people that Mia had pictured as the Snow Angel, a girl their age hadn't even been on the list. The girl had beautiful twists of hair that bounced a little with each step.

"You're the Snow Angel," Lulu said, this time keeping her voice at a whisper.

TWENTY-FIVE

I'm going to tell you about the Snow Angel," the girl said. "But you have to promise not to tell anyone. Not anyone."

"Why?" Mia asked.

The girl leaned back on her heels and crossed her arms. "Do you promise or not?"

"Yes, yes, we promise," Mia said.

The girl narrowed her eyes. "Doesn't sound like a real promise to me."

"Well, how are we supposed to make a promise when we don't even know what you're going to tell us?" Mia said.

"How am I supposed to trust you if you don't?" the girl asked.

"I'm Maddie," Maddie said, speaking up for the first time. "This is my sister Mia. We're twins, even though it's hard to tell by looking. And that's Lulu. We're good at keeping secrets, unless they're the kind that shouldn't be kept."

Mia eyed Lulu, wondering if this was actually true. Lulu wasn't good at keeping secrets, was she?

"Girls, are you okay?" Miss Julia asked, coming over to check on them.

"We're fine," Mia said. "Just making a new friend."

They couldn't talk with Miss Julia standing there, since the girl seemed hesitant to even tell the secret to the girls. Miss Julia took the situation in, noticing the uncomfortable quiet that had settled.

"All right, then," she said. "I'll be right over there on the bench waiting for you, got it?"

"Got it," Maddie said.

Miss Julia watched from a safe distance, giving them enough room to whisper without being overheard. Mia was glad Miss Julia trusted them enough to let them finish their conversation. Maybe she'd heard what Lulu had said about the Snow Angel.

"Do you think she heard?" the girl asked.

"Probably not," Mia said.

"Are you the Snow Angel?" Lulu repeated, bouncing on her toes.

"My name is Shantell Simmons. I'm the forty-second Snow Angel."

"The forty—" Lulu began, forgetting to keep her voice down.

This time all the other girls shushed her.

Lulu put her hands up in apology. "The forty-second? What does that mean?"

Shantell glanced over her shoulder again, and then leaned in toward them, eyes sparkling. "It's a secret society. So far, it's only kids, and it's supposed to be top, top secret. We're not supposed to get caught."

When she said "get caught," her eyes stopped sparkling and her face fell. Mia could tell she felt badly about having been seen.

"We really do promise we won't tell," she told Shantell.

"What do you mean, 'so far'?" Maddie asked.

"In New York, it's impossible not to be seen, because there are so many people around all the time," Shantell said. "But the thing is, adults don't pay much attention to kids, at least when the kids aren't their own. So, we've been able to keep the secret. When someone catches us—so far that's only been kids—we share the secret. And then those kids can be Snow Angels too."

Lulu's eyes were round as saucers. "So we can be Snow Angels?"

Just moments ago, Mia had been thinking about what she'd do if she were a Snow Angel. And now, she could be one!

"There are rules," Shantell said.

"Keep it secret," Lulu said.

"Right. And leave a snowflake with each gift."

"A certain kind of snowflake?" Maddie asked.

Shantell flashed a brilliant smile. "That's the excellent thing about snowflakes. Each one is unique. You have to think hard about the gift. It's not just about leaving whatever for whoever. You want to try to give people something that will mean something to them."

"You left a blanket," Mia said. "Which she clearly needed."

"I chose a bright green one," Shantell said. "Because when I walked by the other day, I heard her tell a man passing by that what she loves most are green M&Ms. He had tried to give her some granola." Again, that bright smile. "So, of course, I left a whole Ziploc full of green M&Ms. I've been sorting them ever since I heard her say she loved them. But I also left her some fruit and a few energy bars in that bag. You can't live on M&Ms alone."

"True," Mia agreed.

"If anyone catches you, you're supposed to invite them to be a Snow Angel too. I guess you're the forty-third, fourth, and fifth . . ." She frowned. "No one really knows, I guess, since other people could have been adding Snow Angels all this time too. It's not like we keep a list or anything. You can give gifts for as long as you want, or just one. But the main thing is keeping this all top, top secret."

"Shantell!" her mom called. "Time to go."

"I've got to go," she told the girls. "Here's the last thing. The first Snow Angel—I don't know her name, but I do know she was a girl—she asked each Snow Angel to pass this on to new Snow Angels. It's from the book *A Little Princess*. It goes like this: 'Though there may be times when your hands are empty, your heart is always full, and you can give things out of that.' You try saying it."

The girls tried repeating it, and Shantell helped them when they forgot words. Finally, they could recite the line on their own.

Shantell gave them the thumbs-up. "Yep. It's not about how much you can give—it's about doing what-ever you can with love."

"Wait!" Mia said, as Shantell turned to go. "That's it? Now we're Snow Angels?"

Shantell grinned. "That's it. Go and Snow Angel it up!"

She ran back toward her mom, leaving the Glimmer girls a little shocked, but each wearing delighted grins.

Finally, Lulu broke the silence by spinning and then starting to prance around in the snow. "Yes, yes, yes!"

"I can't believe it," Maddie said.

"I know," Mia agreed.

"I guess we solved the mystery?" Maddie said.

"Lulu solved the mystery," Mia said. "If she hadn't seen Shantell, we'd never have noticed. It was that quick."

"I hope we can be that quick too," Maddie said, and then shook her head with disbelief. "We're Snow Angels now, Mia!"

Mia could only shake her head, feeling the same disbelief. "I know!"

Excitement fizzed through Mia as she let everything that had just happened sink in.

"Are you girls okay?" Miss Julia asked. "What was that all about?"

The girls looked at each other in alarm. Had Shantell meant they had to keep the secret from everyone? But, no, she couldn't have meant that, since her mom obviously knew what she was up to.

"We'll tell you," Lulu said. "But you can't tell anyone else. Not even Mom and Dad."

"We're not telling Mom and Dad?" Maddie asked.

"Maybe we will later," Mia said. "But we can't tell everyone. Or anyone, actually, other than Miss Julia, and if we think we should, Mom and Dad."

"I think we should," Maddie said.

Miss Julia watched all this as though it were a ping-pong match, her expression growing more and more puzzled. "What's going on, girls?"

"We just figured out who the Snow Angel is," Mia said, grinning.

"Who?" Miss Julia asked, and then looked at where the girl had gone. "Wait, that girl was the Snow Angel?"

"Yep," Mia said, trying to hold back the smile that kept wanting to break through. "And so are we now."

Miss Julia did a double take. "Wait. What?"

The girls burst into peals of laughter and then explained it all to Miss Julia, who finally said, "I can't believe it!"

"Will you help us?" Mia asked. "We'll need to secretly buy some gifts."

"Absolutely," Miss Julia said. "And I do think we should tell your Mom and Dad. But we can do it when we're back in the hotel room, where we can keep it all to ourselves."

TWENTY-SIX

Even the excitement of riding the elevator up to the *Rise and Shine* studio didn't drown out the thrill that filled Mia's whole body. They'd solved the Snow Angel mystery, and now, she was a Snow Angel! It was even better than being on television, and that was saying something.

Jennifer greeted the Glimmer family and Miss Julia at the elevator.

"Welcome! And hello, Lulu." She reached out to shake Lulu's hand.

"Hello!" Lulu said, smiling and on her best behavior.

Mom introduced Dad and Miss Julia, and Jennifer shook their hands.

"The soundstage is this way," Jennifer said, leading them across the studio. "We've got three microphones set up for you, and the piano behind for backup."

"That's for me." Dad took his place at the piano. "What do you say we run through the song, girls?"

Mia, Maddie, and Lulu went to stand by their microphones. Neither Maddie nor Mia argued when Lulu took the center microphone. Like Mom had said in their concert at the Opry, the stage picture looked better with her in the middle. And anyway, "Sun Breaks Through" was Lulu's song. Mom helped the girls adjust their

Natalie Grant

microphone heights and then sat in the audience to listen.

Dad started into the music, and Lulu began to tap her toe and sing, with Mia and Maddie adding harmony and backup vocals. As Lulu sang, she alternated between looking at Mia and then at Maddie, smiling and including them. Mia wondered who had swapped her little sister for someone else. But then they got to Lulu's favorite part in the bridge, and she began to do her Lulu dance thing, totally taking center stage and hamming it up. Mia and Maddie caught each other's eyes and only just kept from rolling their eyes. This was more like the Lulu they knew. Fortunately, Lulu didn't knock over any of the microphones with her swinging arms. Dad pushed the volume and tempo, adding a crescendo as they moved toward the climax of the song. Then, he pulled off as they all wound down, quieting, for the last few notes.

Jennifer, Mom, and even a few members of the camera crew burst into applause.

"Nice work, girls. I have a few sound adjustments. And Lulu . . ." Mom tilted her head. "Maybe a little less arm swinging?"

Lulu gave an apologetic smile. "Sorry about that."

Mom talked to the soundboard operator, and then the girls tried the song a couple more times. Soon, everyone agreed it was just right. It felt right—all the Glimmer girls singing together. Even after all the

difficulty this week, Mia was glad they'd included Lulu. The Sparkle and Shine album might belong to Mia and Maddie and Ruby, but the week in New York felt like it belonged to the Glimmer girls. Especially now that they were Snow Angels, part of the network of secret gift givers. They'd joined an actual secret society.

"We need a handshake," Mia said.

"We do!" Maddie agreed.

"You need what?" Mom asked.

"Nothing," Mia said, catching Maddie's and then Lulu's eyes. Especially here in the studio, they needed to be careful not to let the secret slip.

"Thank you so much, girls," Jennifer said, shaking each of their hands. "We can't wait for your concert tomorrow."

She turned to Mom and Dad. "We've left an open slot in our schedule for the Snow Angel tomorrow. We're hoping he or she will show up tomorrow to reveal the secret. Wouldn't that be the perfect end to Light Up New York Week?"

Mia tensed, sure that Lulu would burst out with something that would give their secret away. But amazingly, impossibly, she stayed silent.

Dad's brow furrowed "Aren't you afraid that people will come out of the woodwork? An open call for a stranger to come on the show? How do you know you won't have a bunch of imposters show up?"

"We'll be screening people," Jennifer said. "But you're right. It could be a big mess. We're hoping people will be honest. The whole point of this week is helping others. We'll see."

Mom, Dad, and Jennifer led the way toward the door, deep in conversation. The girls followed. Mia kept thinking about the secret handshake, trying to come up with the perfect idea.

"Do you think the Snow Angel will show up tomorrow?" one of the camera crew asked as the girls passed.

Mia glanced at Lulu, wondering if her sister had heard, and if now she would blurt out the truth. It seemed too good to be true that she'd held it in for so long. Lulu studied the two men at the camera, and Mia imagined she could hear the gears in her sister's head turning. What fun it would be to whisper, "I know who the Snow Angel is." In fact, Mia felt the tiniest bit tempted herself. But they'd promised to keep the secret, and if she had anything to say about it, they'd keep their promise.

Lulu passed the cameras by, and again, she didn't say anything. She didn't say anything as they said good-bye to Jennifer, or as they rode downstairs in the elevator. She didn't even say anything as they went outside to the cab.

So, Lulu had sung without losing control, and she'd managed to keep the Snow Angel secret. Mia couldn't quite believe it.

"Nice work, Lulu," she said, impressed, as she climbed into the cab next to her little sister.

"Thanks," Lulu said, looking proud of herself.

Mia showed her sisters her idea for their handshake, and they each added a move to it on the way home.

"What's the handshake for?" Dad wanted to know.

"It's a secret," Lulu said, and she looked so full of the secret that Mia was sure she'd spill it right then. She eyed the cab driver. No, they couldn't tell Mom and Dad here. The only safe place was back in the hotel room where no one would overhear.

"We'll tell you soon," Mia said, enjoying the curious looks on Mom and Dad's faces.

TWENTY-SEVEN

B ack in the room, they finally told Mom and Dad the secret.

"Amazing," Dad said.

"And you didn't tell anyone at the studio, even when they were talking about it?" Mom asked. "Nice work, girls!"

Afterward, they took out the paper they'd bought with Miss Julia. They'd planned to make snowflakes just for fun, but now they had a real reason to make them. They were Snow Angels! Mia could still hardly believe it.

"What should the snowflakes look like?" Maddie picked up her paper and studied it. "I mean, do you think they're all exactly like the one we got from Ruthie?"

"Every snowflake is unique," Mia said. "So, I think ours can each be the way we want them to be."

"Can we leave more than one snowflake?" Lulu asked. "Or would that give away that there is more than one of us?"

"I don't think the Snow Angel has ever left more than one snowflake," Mia said. "But maybe we can give away three gifts."

"Oooh, that's a great idea!" Lulu said, and then frowned at her paper. "But how do you turn it into a snowflake?"

"First, you fold it in quarters, like this," Mia said, demonstrating. "And then you can cut the top to make it round. And then maybe fold it again."

"And then, you cut shapes into the fold," Maddie said, cutting a half circle and then a triangle. She unfolded the snowflake to show Lulu. Her half circle turned into a full circle and repeated itself around the snowflake. The triangle turned into a series of diamonds.

"I can do that!" Lulu started folding her paper.

Maddie refolded hers and added more shapes. Mia started cutting too, making sure to add some interesting details to the outer part of the snowflake as well, transforming it from a simple circle into a more complicated snowflake shape.

"So, if we're going to give three gifts, what will they be?" Maddie asked. "We don't know people in New York . . . and the Snow Angel always gives specific gifts."

"What if . . ." Mia said, a plan starting to take shape in her mind. "What if we give our gifts tonight at the concert in Times Square? We know most of the people there will be homeless, right? So, we could give gifts like blankets or other helpful items, and we'd know they'd be useful no matter who we gave them to."

"Or maybe . . ." Maddie said. "We could choose gifts that are special in some way, and then while we're there, we could look for the perfect person to give each to."

"I like that idea even better," Mia said. "What kind of special gifts were you thinking? Like the necklace you gave Ruby?"

"Well, this is a little different," Maddie admitted. "We don't know these people at all, so . . . maybe a book you love, Mia? Or I could give someone drawing pencils and a sketchbook?"

"And I could give someone my detective kit," Lulu said.

"Are you sure . . ." Mia began, wondering what homeless teen would want a toy detective kit. But she stopped herself, realizing that for Lulu to give up her kit, something she had grown completely attached to, her sister was making a huge sacrifice. Maybe it wasn't so much what the gift was, but what it meant to the giver.

"I still think we should give a gift that will be meaningful," Mia said. "I mean, to someone we're more connected to. Or at least someone who we know about. Like how Shantell heard the woman talk about loving green M&Ms."

"But we don't live here, and we only have tomorrow. And then we're going home," Maddie said. "We might just have to do our best, since there's so little time. It's not like we can rush out and buy something after we see the people tomorrow night. We will be too busy with the concert."

"True," Mia said, but her mind wasn't totally with Maddie. A new idea was starting to form, and as it did, her excitement grew along with it. "I have an idea."

"What kind of idea?" Lulu asked.

"You know how the Snow Angel—or one of them—gave a gift to Ruthie on the tour bus and to Diane at the library?"

"Yeah?" Maddie asked, catching Mia's excitement.

"Well, why do you think the Snow Angel gave gifts to them? It's not like they're poor, especially, or anything."

"Because they needed something," Lulu said, her answer immediate and unquestioning. "I don't think the Snow Angels think too much about who has a lot and who has a little. It's more about helping people no matter who they are, right?"

"So, what if instead of giving blankets or something generic, what if we gave the story we made up to the artist who made the snow globe?" Mia asked. "We nearly figured out the whole thing already. She made all those snow globes and is giving all the money she earns from them away. And it seems like . . . well, people who give a lot sometimes don't get anything in return."

"I'm sure she doesn't expect anything in return," Maddie said.

"Do you think she'd like to receive our story about her snow globe in the mail, along with a snowflake?"

Maddie nodded and then frowned. "But wouldn't that give it away, that we are the Snow Angels? I mean, we're the only ones who saw that snow globe."

"Us and everyone in the city of New York," Mia pointed out. "Jennifer held it up on camera for everyone to see. It's possible the Snow Angel would have seen it and written a story about it. You never know."

"I like it," Lulu said, clapping her hands.

"I like that it's something only we can give," Maddie said.

"That way, if we don't have a chance to give anything away at the concert, we can still be Snow Angels."

"True," Maddie said, and then added, "I think we should do it. We should write the story, and that can be our first Snow Angel gift."

"We can always be Snow Angels when we get back home too," Lulu suggested. "We'll have two extra snowflakes."

Being Snow Angels at home hadn't occurred to Mia. As she considered it, she realized they'd have to be extremely careful so no one found them out. But Lulu was right. Nothing was stopping them from continuing the Snow Angel campaign at home, and maybe even spreading it around Nashville. Who knew? Maybe other kids had visited New York and already taken the idea back home with them to their own cities. Mia liked the thought of Snow Angels spreading across the country. An always-growing secret society focused on helping others.

"Should we start now?" she asked, taking out her journal.

"Let's do it!" Maddie said.

"It should start, 'On a dark and snowy night . . .' " Lulu suggested.

Mia wrote this down, and they were off, adding sentence after sentence, filling the page and spilling over onto the next and the next.

TWENTY-EIGHT

The girls set up on the soundstage during a commercial break. Mia gave her sisters a silent high five. This morning, they'd be singing on television. Television! Singing at the Opry had been one kind of special, because so many performers had sung there before. But there was something about performing live on TV, where anyone in the world could be watching. As she thought this, she realized there was definitely a downside. Anyone in the world could be watching, which meant that if they messed up, their mess-up would be broadcast to the world. Plus, once a performance was filmed, it lived on forever.

Breathe, she told herself.

Then, she realized she was trying to do things on her own again. She wondered why her first impulse when she was worried wasn't to pray. It was so easy to forget that God was right there, waiting for her to reach out. *God, please help me*, she prayed silently. *Help us. Help us to sing beautifully. Not so people are impressed, but so we can point people's hearts toward you. And so we can help many teens with the funds raised through sales.*

Maddie gripped Mia's hand. "Whatcha doing?"

"Praying," Mia answered.

"Good idea." Maddie closed her eyes for a moment. When she opened them, she looked much more settled.

Before Mia had any more time to think, the cameras were rolling in their direction and the heat of the lights hit her face. She wasn't sure if she was already on camera, but she smiled anyway, just in case. Across the studio in the living room area, Jennifer welcomed the viewers. She introduced the Glimmer girls as the youngest performers ever to be on the *Rise and Shine* soundstage. Then, she explained the mission of their Sparkle and Shine album.

Near the end of her commentary, from behind Mia, Dad started to play quietly, leading into the song. Had Mia not known about his earpiece, she would have been completely puzzled about how he knew when to start. The tempo and volume rose, and it was time. Lulu began to sing. As the rhythm kicked in and Mia felt the song sweep her along, a smile spread across her face. On the other side of the bright lights, she could see Mom and Miss Julia smiling. The crowd was smiling too. Many people moved in time with the music.

This song, "Sun Breaks Through," was an original that Dad had helped the girls write. It was perfect for Lulu—fast-moving and joy-filled—the kind of song that made you want to dance. Lulu completely threw herself into the song, but also remembered what Mom said about not flailing her arms. Like in rehearsal, she glanced at her two sisters often, including them, and drawing them further into the song with her.

Light Up New York

In spite of the fact that they were on camera, performing for anyone who chose to tune in, Mia felt herself relax in a way she hadn't all week. It felt like letting out a breath she hadn't known she was holding. Maybe things didn't always go the way she wished they would between her and her sisters. Still, sometimes, in moments like this, she caught glimpses of what it could be like. What she and her sisters could be like, if they chose to be. In a way, it was so simple, all of them choosing at the same time to band together, to be there for one another. To not make selfish choices, as Mom might say. But in another way, finding moments like these, when they all did choose to be kind at the same time . . . sometimes that unspoken agreement felt like the most difficult place in the world to reach.

The music began to rise in the final crescendo, and Mia pushed all her thoughts aside. Right now, all that mattered was the music. Just this moment. The melody seemed to take on its own weight and texture in the air around her, filling the room with joy. And then it was over, and the audience members were on their feet, clapping. She and her sisters took their bow. Then, the girls motioned to Dad, who waved and then winked at the girls. Mia could see he was proud. His pride in them was the cherry on top of the whole experience.

Jennifer was standing too, clapping. She crossed the studio to join the girls on the soundstage.

"What a performance," she said, to renewed cheers and applause from the crowd. Once the noise had quieted, Jennifer said to the camera, "Now, remember, when you purchase the Sparkle and Shine album, you're supporting homeless teens. So, not only will you be enjoying excellent music by these talented girls, but you'll also be supporting an important cause."

"And Ruby too," Maddie added. "Ruby was actually the one with the idea for the album, and she sings on every song except this one."

Jennifer turned to the camera and smiled. "Ruby, if you're watching, I want to say a special thank you to you. What a wonderful idea you had. Thank you for the gifts you're giving to the community." She turned back to the girls. "Now, girls, can you tell me why you call this album Sparkle and Shine?"

"We have a family motto," Lulu said. "Glimmer girls sparkle and shine, but most of all, they are kind."

"Wonderful," Jennifer said. "Wonderful. Now we're just about out of time, but before we go, I wonder if you can help us out, girls. Our next slot was supposed to be for the Snow Angel, and try as we might, we haven't been able to find him or her. We wonder, do you have a theory on who the Snow Angel might be?"

Mia couldn't have been more surprised if Jennifer had reached down and pulled the rug out from under their feet. Did Jennifer know? She couldn't. But then why was she asking them this question? Mia's heart thumped in her chest, and the silent words, *Don't do it, Lulu. Don't do it!* beat in her ears. But how could she expect her little sister to keep the secret at a moment like this, with the eyes of . . . everyone . . . watching?

Mia knew she should say something, but she wasn't sure what to say. Should she lie on national television? No, of course she shouldn't. But what should she do?

"I guess," Lulu said finally, making Mia cringe. She shouldn't have left the reply up to her little sister. She really shouldn't have. "I guess the Snow Angel wants to keep her . . . or his . . . secret."

Mia's head whipped around, and she stared at Lulu in shock. Lulu smiled, a smile that reminded Mia of the stone cat's mysterious smile from the museum yesterday.

Jennifer shook her head and shrugged regretfully. "I guess you're right, Lulu." She turned out to the cameras. "Well, New York, I guess it's up to you, then. When we come back, we'll hit the streets and ask you for your theories, since we can't hear from the Snow Angel him- or herself. And maybe one day, the mystery will be solved."

After this, the lights began to slowly decrease in intensity, and the cameras rolled away.

"Girls, that was astounding," Jennifer said, hugging each of them in turn. "Thank you so much."

There wasn't much time to linger onstage, because Jennifer had to move to her living room stage again and prepare for the next segment of the show. Dad and the girls went backstage, where Mom and Miss Julia were waiting.

"Girls, you were incredible. I'm so proud of you," Mom said, and then leaned in close to whisper to Lulu. "And you didn't tell. Wow!"

"I know," Mia said.

"Lulu, you're the best," Maddie said.

Then, everyone started hugging everyone else, until Mia wasn't sure how many times she'd hugged anyone. She started to laugh, and soon they were all laughing. Laughing their way out of the studio. Breaking into laughter again every time they caught one another's eyes in the elevator. Even laughing as they climbed into the cab. When they arrived at the hotel, Mia's stomach hurt from laughing so much, but still she couldn't stop.

TWENTY-NINE

Before the concert that night, the girls slipped their finished story along with Mia's snowflake into a thick white envelope. Mia had won two rounds of rock-paper-scissors, making hers the one they chose. They agreed to save Maddie and Lulu's snowflakes for Snow Angel missions back home in Nashville. With Miss Julia, they took the envelope down to Grand Central Terminal to drop into the mailbox. So many people passed through Grand Central, it seemed the perfect place to post their mysterious letter.

While they'd been at *Rise and Shine* that morning, Miss Julia had asked a receptionist for Thea Vance's address. She'd explained that the girls wanted to send a thank-you note for the snow globe. Mia suggested they should send the thank you after they arrived home. Thea would receive her thank you from Nashville and hopefully never connect the girls with the Snow Angel envelope. Plus, they'd printed and bound the story in the hotel's business center. Mia hadn't expected it to come out looking so professional, but their finished book looked elegant. Maybe Thea would suspect the story was written by children, but maybe she wouldn't. In any case, she hoped their Snow Angel secret was safe.

The girls couldn't wear dresses for the concert that night, since they'd be singing outside in the cold. Fortunately for everyone who was sleeping outside, the snow had stopped. The temperature hovered around 40 degrees, which was very cold, but still warmer than it had been all week. The girls bundled up in sweaters and tights, and then pulled on their hats, gloves, and scarves.

"We don't look very sparkly," Lulu said, eyeing her outfit in the mirror.

"You'll be happy you have those hats and gloves when you've been outside for a little bit," Miss Julia said. "I'm bringing the blankets too. When you're not singing, you'll probably want to watch the concert, and it will be cold."

In the end, Mia didn't feel much of the cold, really. When they arrived in Times Square, everyone bustled around, setting up, welcoming people, passing out votive candles. Covenant House set up a station for anyone who needed blankets, coats, socks, gloves, or hats. Everyone involved in the sleep-out was directed to gather a few blocks from Times Square. Mia could see it was a good mix of people who'd chosen to sleep out as part of the event and others who had no choice but to sleep out on the streets. Tonight, whether you had a fancy house or nothing at all, you were the same as everyone else. Just a person, sleeping out on the hard concrete, surviving the cold. When the concert began, everyone would light their candles and stream into the Square, filling the space with light. Mia couldn't wait to see it.

Backstage, there was an area for the performers to gather, with heat lamps and hot tea, coffee, and hot cocoa. Lulu would have filled her entire mug with marshmallows, but Miss Julia noticed in time and gave the girls a limit of three each. Good thing, or their song might have been a sugar-high disaster, Mia thought. Excitement sparked backstage as performers arrived and the time for the concert approached.

"It would have been impossible to do the . . ." Maddie glanced over her shoulder to see if anyone was listening, and then raised her eyebrows to say, "You know. Tonight."

"Yeah, I'm glad we chose the story," Mia said.

"Shhh!" Lulu hushed them.

Mia grinned. "It's okay. No one knows what we're talking about. And no one's listening."

"I didn't think we were going to solve this one," Maddie said. "I thought we'd have to break our mystery-solving streak, for sure."

"And we wouldn't have solved the mystery if you hadn't spotted Shantell, Lulu," Mia added.

Lulu gave a little curtsy. "You're welcome. It was probably because I had the detective kit. Thanks to you."

"Girls, do you want to go around the side to see the candles?" Mom asked. "I'll be up on stage, but Miss Julia can take you around to watch and then make sure you're backstage in time for your song."

"Yes, yes, yes!" Lulu said, clapping her hands.

"Yes!" Mia echoed. She'd been waiting all week to see the candles. It was Light Up New York Week, after all.

Mom kissed each of them, and then headed for the stage. Miss Julia led them out of the backstage area. The crew had set up a small platform off to the side where people could see the stage and the entire Square. Mia looped her arm through Maddie's as the band struck the first chord. Soon, music filled Times Square.

"Look!" Maddie pointed to the far distance, where pinpricks of light could now be seen. As the crowd slowly approached, with people holding their votives out in front of them, the light crowded out the darkness. Soon, Times Square flickered and glowed, filled with light and warmth and people.

"What do you think it would feel like," Maddie asked, "if you lived on the streets, and you were cold and lonely, and then you saw . . . this?"

Mia blinked hard, tears prickling at the corners of her eyes. "I think I'd start to have hope. At least a little bit. I'd start to hope things could be better."

"Me too," Maddie said.

"Me three," Lulu piped up, pushing her way into the middle.

They relinked arms, with Lulu in the middle. The girls stood, letting the music wash over them, watching the candle flames flicker and dance.

"They lit up New York," Maddie said, as the song ended.

"They did," Mia agreed.

"Are you ready to go sing, girls?" Miss Julia asked.

"Time to sparkle and shine!" Lulu said.

"Time to sparkle and shine," Mia and Maddie echoed, the light of hundreds of flames dancing in their eyes.

London Art Chase

*By Award-Winning Recording
Artist Natalie Grant*

In *London Art Chase*, the first title in
the new Faithgirlz Glimmer Girls series,
readers meet 10-year-old twins Mia and
Maddie and their adorable little sister,
Lulu. All the girls are smart, sassy, and
unique in their own way, each with a spe-
cial little something that adds to great family adventures.

There is pure excitement in the family as the group heads to
London for the first time to watch mom, famous singer Gloria
Glimmer, perform. But on a day trip to the National Gallery,
Maddie witnesses what she believes to be an art theft and takes
her sisters and their beloved and wacky nanny, Miss Julia, on a
wild and crazy adventure as they follow the supposed thief to his
lair. Will the Glimmer Girls save the day? And will Maddie find
what makes her shine?

Available in stores and online!

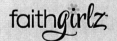

A Dolphin Wish

By Award-Winning Recording Artist Natalie Grant

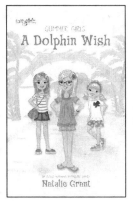

Join twins Mia and Maddie and their sidekick little sister, Lulu, as they travel the country finding adventure, mystery, and sometimes mischief along the way. Together with their famous mother, singer Gloria Glimmer, and their slightly wacky nanny Miss Julia, the sisters learn lessons about being good friends, telling the truth, and a whole lot more.

In *A Dolphin Wish*—a three-night stop in the city of San Diego seems like it might be just the break the girls need—lovely weather and great sights to see. That is until they hear animal handlers at Captain Swashbuckler's Adventure Park talking about the trouble they've been having keeping the animals in their habitats. Mia and her sisters cannot resist a challenge and they talk Miss Julia into another visit to the educational amusement park to search for clues as to what or who is helping the animals escape.

Available in stores and online!

Glimmer Girls

Miracle in Music City

By Award-Winning Recording Artist Natalie Grant

In *Miracle in Music City*, the third title in the Faithgirlz Glimmer Girls series by Natalie Grant, the Glimmer Girls are at it again—looking for a mystery to solve. Gloria wants her daughters to learn they aren't too young to make a difference, so she gets them involved in her annual benefit and auction. But as things often do with the trio of smart and sassy sisters, Maddie, Mia, and Lulu get themselves and their nanny Miss Julia involved in a lot more than just helping Mom raise money for a worthy and wonderful cause.

Available in stores and online!

CPSIA information can be obtained
at www.ICGtesting.com
Printed in the USA
LVOW08s1931011217
558333LV00008B/48/P